MW00585659

DAWN LEE MCKENNA'S

SQUALL LINE

A *FORGOTTEN COAST* SUSPENSE NOVEL: BOOK NINE

SWEET TEA PRESS

2018

A SWEET TEA PRESS PUBLICATION

First published in the United States by Sweet Tea Press

©2018 Dawn Lee McKenna. All rights reserved.

Edited by Debbie Maxwell Allen

Cover by Shayne Rutherford
wickedgoodbookcovers.com

Interior Design by Colleen Sheehan
ampersandbookinteriors.com

Squall Line is a work of fiction. All incidents and dialogue, and all characters, are products of the author's imagination. Any similarities to any person, living or dead, is merely coincidental.

for

all our law enforcement officers; those still with us,

and those who are not

ONE

yan Warner felt for the light switch, flicked it on, and watched as, row by row, the ancient fluorescent tubes came to life. They started with the front of the room, over Mr. Carpenter's desk, then made their way, flickering and popping, over six rows of lab tables. It was late Thursday afternoon, last period, and the sky outside the room's two windows was overcast.

Each table was covered in black Corian and had three high stools on each side. In the center of each were caddies filled with forceps, long tweezers, and other tools of dissection and discovery.

Along the back wall was a bank of cabinets that ran the whole width of the room. The cabinets held locked boxes of scalpels and other sharp objects, formalin, cotton balls and swabs, and many other items frequently used in the 9th-to-12th grade biology lab.

On the countertop that covered these cabinets were several cages, and those cages came to life as the lights came on fully and Ryan made his way between two rows of lab tables toward the back of the room.

"Hey, you guys," Ryan said softly. In the closest of the cages, two gray and white rats stuck their faces up against the side, pink noses and white whiskers quivering. Mr. Carpenter, the biology teacher, gave Ryan a library pass on Fridays in exchange for feeding the animals during his study hall period the rest of the week. Ryan was always ahead in class anyway, and Mr. Carpenter knew that Ryan was planning on being a vet.

Ryan reached into the outside pocket of his backpack and pulled out a plastic bag of carrot ends, apple cores, lettuce leaves, and other scraps his mom saved for him.

At seventeen, Ryan was shorter and slighter than most of the other senior boys. He stood only five foot five and wasn't involved in any team sports, nor was he interested in going to a gym. He liked books, and he liked animals.

He was a good-looking boy, in a nerdy way, with deep-brown hair and black hipster glasses, but if any of the girls at school found him attractive, he was too shy and too distracted to know about it. He did his work, ate his lunch with a few other kids that were new, nerdy or otherwise left to the fringes of school society, and went home to lose himself in his books, or connect online with his friends from back home in Orlando, kids he'd grown up with. They were all nerds or geeks, too, but they knew him and accepted him.

His dad had died two years ago, and after a year of trying to support them on one income, Ryan's mother had made the decision to move here to Eastpoint, FL, where she had family and the cost of living was a bit lower. Ryan hated it, and he was glad his first year of school in Eastpoint was also his last.

He didn't mind living there; he loved being across the bay from the beach. He thought Apalach, across the bridge, was a cool little town, and he liked being closer to his relatives. He just hated the school. More accurately, he hated the way he was constantly afraid there. Adrian Nichols and his buddies had made Ryan's life a living hell all year.

There were only two weeks left of school, and then he would be free. He'd spent the last four years fervently believing that he would fit in better at college than he had in high school. In August, he would be back in Orlando, where he'd registered at UCF. They had a great veterinary program and he had a full scholarship, so maybe his mom could quit one of her jobs.

Milo's was the last cage in the line. Milo was a white rat, and Ryan's favorite. He had just filled Milo's water bottle and was scratching him under the chin when he heard the classroom door *thunk* closed on its hydraulic hinges. Expecting to see either Mr. Carpenter or some teacher wondering why the lights were on, Ryan looked over his shoulder and felt like his intestines were crawling toward his feet. It was Adrian Nichols and his faithful followers.

Adrian wasn't a whole lot taller than Ryan, but he was a good deal stockier, and most of it was muscle. He was a varsity wrestler and also worked on his dad's shrimp boat. With sun-bleached blond hair and a deep tan, he seemed to be pretty popular with the girls. He had also collected a small group of minions, guys who weren't as good-looking or as popular.

Drake Woods was a wrestler, too, but he had close-set eyes and a horrible case of acne. Stuart Newman was forty pounds overweight. Brian Gentry was just socially awkward, and his sparse blond goatee didn't do much for his looks.

Ryan watched them as they approached, so focused on Adrian's mean smirk that he ignored Milo's playful nibbles on his palm.

"Lookee here," Adrian said. "Cryin' Ryan's hanging out with all the other lab rats."

"No wonder it always smells in here," Drake said.

Ryan tried not to swallow as the boys advanced. He felt trapped, like a fish in one of those woven fish baskets, wondering why it couldn't get out the same way it got in.

"That your girlfriend?" Adrian asked, his eyes flicking to Milo and back to Ryan.

Ryan had forgotten his hand was still in the cage, and he yanked it out and reached for the door.

"Ah-ah-ah," Adrian said, wagging his finger at Ryan. "Let's see here."

"We're not supposed to handle them except in class," Ryan blurted, as Adrian's big hand reached for the cage door that Ryan was trying to close.

"Really?" Adrian asked as he shoved Ryan's hand out of the way. Ryan felt a sudden nausea as Adrian reached into the cage and picked up Milo. The rat shied a bit, but he was used to being held and didn't bite. Ryan wished he would, as Adrian held him up in his palm. "You mean like this?"

"Gross, man," the portly Stuart said. "They carry diseases."

"Or like this?" Adrian asked, ignoring Stuart and lifting Milo up by his tail.

It startled Milo and made him nervous. He let out a quick, quiet squeak, and arched his back in a futile attempt to right himself.

"Stop it!" Ryan said. "Come on, leave him alone."

"He wants to play," Adrian said.

"Hey, man," Stuart said, pulling out his phone and turning on the camera. "See if you can get him to do some tricks."

Ryan felt panic creeping from his gut to his throat. Panic and rage. He couldn't abide animal cruelty, and Milo was his friend. "Come on. Please," Ryan said shakily. "Just give him back."

Adrian ignored him, looking over his shoulder at Stuart the cameraman. Stuart and Adrian imagined themselves the next YouTube stars, and were constantly uploading stuff they hoped would go viral. None of it was educational or otherwise edifying, and much of it was downright brutal or offensive.

"I bet I can make him disappear," Adrian said to Stuart.

Drake, the other wrestler, grinned meanly. "How about a live dissection?"

Adrian and Stuart laughed, but when Ryan glanced over at Brian, who was always the quietest of the bunch, he wasn't smiling. His eyes met Ryan's for just a moment, before he glanced at the floor, then over at his friends.

"Come on, you guys," Brian said nervously. "The rats are cool."

Ryan couldn't help shooting him a look of gratitude, but it was lost on Brian, who was focused on his friends.

"Don't be a weenie, Gentry," Adrian said, frowning. "It's a rat."

Milo had given up squeaking and writhing, and hung beneath Adrian's hand, his only movement the rapid heartbeats jerking his ribcage.

Adrian looked back at Ryan. "How much cash you got on you?"

"What? Nothing," Ryan answered, taken aback.

"That's bull. How much money you have on you?" he asked again, this time wiggling Milo's tail just a bit.

"I mean it," Ryan answered. "I don't have any money on me. My money's at home."

"That's too bad," Adrian said. "For ten bucks, I'd let him go."

"I can get you ten bucks," Ryan said, trying not to sound too eager, or too afraid.

"Nope. Cash in hand," Adrian said. "Ten bucks is pretty cheap to keep me from squeezing his head right off."

Ryan suddenly felt truly nauseous. Milo was a help-less animal, an intelligent and affectionate one, and he was Ryan's friend.

"Come on, man," Brian interjected, more quietly this time.

"Shut up, Brian," Adrian said without looking at him. He held Milo up to his eye level. "You guys only live a couple of years, anyway, right?"

Milo twisted around to see Adrian, and Adrian tucked a finger under the rat's chin. Frightened, Milo gave his finger a nip. Adrian cursed, and Ryan's heart sank.

"You want to play, you little jerk?" Adrian yelled at the rat.

As Adrian raised his free hand, to do something Ryan couldn't predict but knew would be bad, Ryan found himself involuntarily launching himself at the larger boy. Catching him unaware, Ryan shoved at his chest.

"Leave him alone!" he yelled.

In his surprise, Adrian let go of Milo's tail, and the rat dropped unharmed to the terrazzo floor and scurried under the cabinet.

When Ryan looked back up at Adrian, his heart started racing even faster. The pure hatred in Adrian's eyes was frightening.

"Buddy, you've just made the worst mistake of your life," Adrian said. "I'm seriously gonna mess you up."

"Do it!" Stuart cheered, still holding up his phone.

"Punk," Drake added.

Ryan risked taking his eyes off Adrian just long enough to glance at Brian, but the other boy wouldn't meet his eyes. His "Let's just go" was the only help he offered.

Adrian took a step toward Ryan, holding his gaze. "I've been nice to you till now," he said evenly. He lifted a fist, and Ryan felt a sudden warmth on his thigh.

"Dude!" Stuart yelled, smiling. "He just pissed hisself."

Adrian had just glanced down at the front of Ryan's pants when the door was roughly pushed open, and all of the boys turned to look. Mr. Carpenter stood there, one hand on his hip. He took in the situation immediately.

"What are you boys doing in here?" he demanded.

"Nothing, sir, just helping Ryan," Adrian said with a smirk.

"He doesn't need your help. You guys have passes?"

"We're on our way to practice," Adrian said.

"Then get there."

Ryan and Carpenter watched as the boys filtered out of the room. Adrian glared at Ryan over his shoulder, and Ryan knew the reprieve would be short.

"You okay, Ryan?" Carpenter asked when they were gone. Ryan saw him see his pants, and his face warmed.

"Yeah," he said. "I have to get Milo."

Carpenter walked across the room as Ryan knelt on all fours and made the clicking noise he used with the rats. After a moment, Milo stuck his nose out, tested the air with his whiskers, and then scurried into Ryan's hand.

"You want me to take you to the principal's office?" Carpenter asked.

"Why? You didn't see anything. She's not going to do anything." Ryan turned away from his teacher to put the rat back into his cage and used the moment to blink back hot tears of frustration and humiliation.

"Ryan."

"I'm okay," Ryan said, closing the cage.

Carpenter sighed. "Come with me to the teacher's lounge," he said quietly. "I have some sweats you can borrow."

CHAPTER

TWO

The next morning, Lt. Maggie Hamilton punched the button on the coffeemaker, grumbling to herself about the fact that she'd forgotten to set the timer the night before.

She and Wyatt had gotten the new coffeemaker as a wedding present back in April, but Maggie hadn't gotten around to opening it until they'd moved just five weeks ago.

They had moved into her childhood home on the bay just outside Apalach, and her parents had moved into her old house, a stilt house on five acres that Daddy's daddy had built. It suited all concerned, but they were still adjusting; figuring out where things went, and then figuring out where they had actually put them. Things like the new coffeemaker that she had managed to learn to use but couldn't remember to set.

She turned away from the counter to grab the milk from the fridge, and nearly tripped over her rooster, Stoopid, who was in the middle of explaining that the seagulls were pooping into the chicken run again, or that he needed her to pick up some Cheetos after work.

"I got it, Stoopid, I got it," Maggie muttered, though she didn't get it any more than usual.

Stoopid tapped along behind her, and when she opened the fridge door, he excitedly implored the scrap bowl to throw itself onto the floor. Maggie grabbed the milk and the scrap bowl and took them to the butcher block island. She took a stainless-steel cat bowl from the island drawer, dumped some vegetable peelings into it, and plunked it onto the floor.

"Shut up," Maggie said without enthusiasm. She loved Stoopid, but she loved a lot of people. Just not before coffee.

She was standing in front of the coffeemaker, waiting for there to be enough to steal, when her seventeen-year-old daughter Sky hurried into the bright kitchen.

"Hey, is that not ready?" Sky asked.

"I forgot to set it."

"Well, crap." Sky blew away a lock of dark-brown hair that hung from the messy bun Maggie had never been able to replicate.

"Why aren't you gone yet?" Maggie asked. "It's almost eight."

"It's a half-day today," Sky answered. "And since I don't have anything but finals reviews left, I'm just studying in the library." Sky was graduating in two weeks as her class valedictorian, then she was off to Florida State. Maggie's chest hurt every time she looked at her.

"Oh. It is it a half-day for Kyle, too?"

"Yeah."

Maggie's son Kyle was going on thirteen, and just finishing up seventh grade. "The busses are running, though, right? Because I've got court this morning, then Dwight's promotion ceremony at one."

"Yeah, the busses are running," Sky said. "He just left."

Maggie stooped to be eye level with the coffeemaker. There was still less than half a cup. "I'm gonna have to go to Kirk's." Maggie visited Kirk Lynch, the owner of Apalachicola Coffee, every day, precisely at 2:45pm, when her internal alarm indicated she would kill somebody and then fall unconscious if she didn't have a *café con leche*. In a morning emergency, such as today's, she had to deal with him twice.

"Oooh, I'm going, too," Sky said, tapping around on her phone. Maggie watched her. People said she was Maggie's double, with her petite frame, long brown hair, and large green eyes, but Maggie thought her daughter gorgeous and herself only marginally pretty.

"Where are you going?" Wyatt asked as he walked into the room, immediately shrinking the large kitchen with his six-foot four frame.

"Kirk's," Sky answered without looking up.

"Oh, I thought you were leaving for college early," Wyatt said, bending to give Maggie a kiss. "I was gonna go ahead and get started on my football room."

"You can have my room soon enough," Sky said, still messing with her phone.

"No, he cannot," Maggie said. "You'll be home at least a couple weekends a month."

"It's okay, I can just sleep with you guys." She looked up at Wyatt. "You guys have probably gotten that out of your system by now, right?"

Wyatt, Maggie's former boss at the Sheriff's office, and her husband of just two months, tossed Sky a look.

"You're a jerk," Wyatt said. He looked at Maggie. "What time is court?"

"Eight-thirty."

"You're going to Kirk's?"

"Yep."

"But the coffee's over there making itself."

"It's not real coffee, and it's not making itself fast enough."

"Well, then I'm going, too."

"What the hell?" Sky said to her phone.

"Sky."

"Sorry, but what is *wrong* with people?" Sky shook her phone.

"What?" Maggie asked, frowning.

Sky heaved a sigh. "Adrian and Stuart. They're jerks, seniors. They posted a video of Ryan Warner peeing his pants."

"Who's Ryan Warner?" Maggie asked.

"He's new. I was his mentor during the first week of school, but I don't really know him that well. But he's a nice guy."

"Who are these other kids?" Wyatt asked.

"They're just jerks. They're bullies," Sky answered.

"And they posted a video of this poor kid?" Maggie popped a fist on her hip.

"Yeah. Omigosh, this is just…it's bull!" Sky stabbed at the phone to close the screen. "I mean, he's a nice kid."

"I don't get it. What was going on? I mean, why'd the kid wet his pants?" Wyatt grabbed his car keys, service weapon and ID from a big blue bowl on the counter. He'd resigned as Sheriff so he could marry Maggie, but he still carried a weapon. He said it was mainly for the reporters. He was now the Public Information Officer for the Sheriff's Office, which was ironic, given the fact that he wasn't crazy about the public and didn't much care for giving information, either.

"I can't really tell, I didn't have the sound on. It looked like they were ganging up on him in one of the classrooms."

"That kid has to be mortified," Maggie said.

"Not to be sexist, but if you were a guy, you'd know mortification was just the beginning. This video's online?" Wyatt asked Sky.

"Yeah, they have a link to it on Facebook."

"Why are you friends with these guys on Facebook?" Maggie asked.

"I'm not, Mom. Bella tagged me. Not to make fun of him, just to say it sucks."

"You know I love Bella but sharing a post like that just spreads it all over the place."

Sky shrugged and shook her head. "It's everywhere anyway."

Maggie sighed as she grabbed her own keys from the bowl and picked up a stack of case files. "I hope Kyle doesn't have to deal with kids like this next year."

"Please, Mom," Sky said, grabbing her backpack from the counter. "Have you seen him lately? He's beautiful. Besides, everybody loves Kyle."

"So what's your schedule?' Wyatt asked Maggie.

"I'm taking Dwight to an early lunch after court, then we'll be at the promotion ceremony."

Maggie looked down as Stoopid began another monologue, his chicken diaper rustling as he followed her to the door.

"Sky, can you take Stoopid's diaper off and shove him out in the run?"

"Oh, Mom, that is so awkward for me."

"Why? It's just chicken poop."

"It's not the poop, it's the fact that I know why you want me to take off his diaper."

"We're gonna run out of chickens if we don't get any fertilized eggs," Maggie said. She looked over at her husband.

"What? I'm not his pimp," he said, slapping his SO ball cap on. "Besides, I feel sorry for him. I think the seagulls pick on him about the diapers."

"That's his problem," Maggie said, shoving the files at him. "He's the one who thinks he should live inside."

She bent and scooped up Stoopid, who protested with a few wing flaps and a smattering of verbal complaints.

"Don't worry about the seagulls," she told him. "They're just jealous."

⚓ ⚓ ⚓

Lynn's Quality Oysters was located in Eastpoint, about a mile or so beyond the bridge that connected Eastpoint to Maggie's home in Apalachicola. Apalach was world famous for its oysters, but many of the oystermen and women lived in Eastpoint. Apalach was a quaint, historic town beloved by tourists, while Eastpoint was mainly working class, and the way to get to the bridge that went out to St. George Island.

Eastpoint was also home to the Franklin County Sheriff's Office, and Lynn's was a favorite haunt of her co-workers, and everyone else she knew. Run by the same family for generations, Lynn's was a wholesaler and seafood market with a few cramped tables inside, and a couple of picnic tables on the back deck, right over the water. Pelicans were the only nod to atmosphere.

Maggie and Dwight Schultz were sitting on the back deck, sipping their sweet teas. Dwight was ten years her junior at twenty-nine, and Maggie had known him most of her life. He was scrawny and sweet, but he'd worked his daddy's shrimp boat since he could walk, and he was stronger than he looked. He was, in fact, the first person in his family to do something other than shrimping, having applied to the Sheriff's Office immediately after graduating high school.

Dwight had married his high school sweetheart, Amy, the day after he'd graduated the academy, and they now scrimped and saved so that she could stay home with their three kids, aged six, four and one. For the last year and a half, Maggie had been mentoring and training Dwight for a promotion to Sergeant and a place in the Criminal Investigative Division. The increase in pay would make a huge difference to Dwight's family, and the added investigator would make a huge difference to Maggie's. She was one of only two investigators with the Sheriff's Office, which served a county of fewer than twenty-five hundred people.

"Anyhow," Dwight was saying, as he picked at what was left of his steamed shrimp, "Amy doesn't know it yet, but I changed our vacation plans for next month."

"That doesn't sound healthy." Maggie squeezed one drop of lemon onto a raw oyster, then tipped her head back and let the cold, salty sweetness slide into her mouth.

"No, I got a surprise for her," Dwight said, his prominent Adam's apple dancing. "I got us a Groupon deal for a hotel up in Fort Walton. Four days. Her mama's gonna take the kids. This is gonna be our first time without the babies."

"That's cool, Dwight. You guys'll love it if you can stop thinking about the kids."

"Yeah, I reckon that could be a problem, but a problem on the beach is better than a problem in our back yard."

He popped his last shrimp into his mouth, and Maggie reached over as a pink shrimp leg landed on his chest. They normally wore jeans or khakis and their SO polo shirts for work, but today Dwight was all fixed up in his full black uniform, his badge polished to a high shine.

"Watch it," Maggie said, picking the shrimp leg off his shirt.

"Aw, crud," Dwight said.

Maggie flicked the leg into his red plastic basket. "Don't worry, it didn't stain."

"Man, Mags, I forgot how long it took to put all this stuff on."

He wiped his mouth with his napkin, looked at his watch, and jumped up from his seat. "Shoot, I gotta run over and get Sophie at the bus stop."

Dwight's oldest daughter was in first grade. They lived just across 98 and back a few blocks, and Dwight was meeting her at the school bus stop so she could ride in his cruiser to the Sheriff's Office. Amy and the younger two would meet them there.

"Go ahead, I'll get this," Maggie said. "Only because it's your big day."

"Thanks. I'll be back in a minute," he said as he hurried off.

⚓   ⚓   ⚓

It was a pain in the neck to get out of the tiny parking lot and then across 98. It was much faster to walk across, so Dwight waited for a break in traffic, then ran across 98 and then up School Road. It was only three blocks, two up and one over, to the bus stop, but Dwight was grateful for the overcast sky and the almost cool breeze from a coming storm. He didn't want to sweat up his uniform.

School Road was lined with working-class homes and mature trees. In some places, old live oaks nearly met over the yellow line.

It only took him two minutes to get to Smith, and as he rounded the corner he saw that the bus was already there, at the next corner, facing away from him. He picked up his step.

There were a couple of middle and high school students already walking away from the bus, looking like pack mules under the bulk of their backpacks. There was also a small group of high school boys standing just a few feet outside the open bus door. The buses carried students from elementary, middle and high school together. Sam, the bus driver, liked to let the older kids off first so they didn't trample the little ones.

For just a second, Dwight thought it was weird that the little kids weren't getting off the bus, but then he realized why, as he heard Sam yell at the boys to move on. It looked like a fight was afoot.

As he hurried closer, Dwight could pick up the conversation.

A kid Dwight didn't know shoved another kid he only knew by sight, the kid that lived with his mom a few blocks away.

"I told you I was gonna mess you up, Warner!" the first kid said. The blond.

"Kick his ass, man!" That was Stuart Newman. Dwight didn't like him, or his daddy.

"Y'all boys get away from the bus stop!" Dwight heard Sam yell. Sam had been the bus driver for this route since Dwight was in sixth grade.

Dwight was just a few yards away when the blond guy shoved the smaller boy in the chest. Dwight had his mouth open to yell when the smaller boy suddenly pulled a .22 out from under his hoodie. Dwight's heart thumped as the kid pointed it at the bigger kid.

"I'm sick and tired of you! Leave me alone!" the smaller kid yelled, pointing the gun at the blonde. His arm was stretched out straight, and Dwight could see his hand shaking.

"Whoa, whoa—" the bully started to yell.

"Hey!" Dwight said, raising his voice but trying to keep it non-threatening. He held his hands up in the air. The boys' heads all jerked in his direction as he reached the group. "Hey now, son," Dwight said to the kid with the gun. The boy's eyes were as big as plates, and there was anger there, but there was more fear.

"Hey," Dwight said again, more quietly. "Come on. I seen these kids pickin' on you. I know you're mad. But don't make a terrible mistake, okay?"

"They have been on me 24/7 for a year!" the kid yelled, his voice breaking from fear and adrenaline. "Why can't I just go to school?"

Dwight took his eyes from the kid's just long enough to glance at the gun. It was a .22 semi-auto, with a four-inch barrel. The slide-mounted safety was off.

"I gotcha. I do," Dwight said softly. "Look at me. I was the smallest guy in my class. The poorest, too. I get it, I promise. But these boys ain't worth what it's gonna do to your life if you pull that trigger, you understand?"

"I'm not trying to shoot anybody," the kid yelled, his voice high and tight. "I just want them to leave me alone!"

Dwight glanced over at the other boys, who stood in a semi-circle. They didn't have anything to say, apparently.

"Dwight, I already done called 911!" Sam yelled.

Dwight had forgotten the bus was there. He looked up at the row of windows and swallowed hard as he saw Sophie staring out at him, her eyes big and frightened.

"Sam?" Dwight called, his eyes back on the boy with the gun. "Sam, you go on. Go on 'round the corner, okay?"

The bus didn't move, but Dwight didn't have time to focus on Sam, or on his little girl.

"Son, what's your name?" Dwight asked the brown-haired boy.

"Ryan." The kid looked scared to death, and he'd lowered his arm so the gun was aimed roughly at the other boy's legs, but his hand shook and the safety was still off.

"Ryan, I know this isn't what you want, this right here," Dwight said. "I see you're scared. I know this is bad and all, but it's not so bad yet that it's gonna change your life, you know what I mean?"

Ryan looked from Dwight to the blond kid and back again.

"Come on, Ryan," Dwight said kindly. "It'll be okay."

"Ryan, we're sorry, man," the skinny kid with a goatee said, his voice shaking.

Dwight glanced over at him. He looked just as scared as Ryan. The other kids looked scared, but not nearly as much. Stuart Newman had pulled a phone out of somewhere and was holding it up, pointed at Ryan. Dwight was about to tell him to put it away when the blond kid tossed his backpack at Ryan's arm.

Ryan saw it coming and started to jump back, but his arm went up reflexively and swung away as though to avoid being hit. Swung away toward Dwight, and before Dwight could even start to believe what might happen, the gun went off.

It seemed like a lot of time went by, between the sound and the pain that Dwight felt in his abdomen. It was like fire and a sledgehammer all at once, and Dwight almost believed it was something other than a bullet, because it just didn't seem like what it would feel like to be shot.

His hearing seemed to fade out, like the time he watched a shrimp boat explode. He could hear kids screaming, but they sounded far away for a second, and then the volume got turned up again. The blond kid was running away, and the little kids…they were screaming so loud, and he could hear Sophie above all of them. He could faintly hear the gears of the door as it unfolded and shut, or maybe he just saw it.

He felt the warmth spreading over his stomach, and he put a hand over it as his eyes met Ryan's. The kid was white as a sheet, but he tore his eyes from Dwight's and started running. Dwight registered a millisecond of disbelief that the big kid was standing there with his phone up in front of his face.

Dwight looked up at the bus, at the window where Sophie's face was, where she was screaming, and calling "Daddy!"

He raised his other arm and waved toward the corner. "Sam, go on! Go on around the corner!"

The bus jumped into motion, and Dwight took a few steps as Sophie plastered her face to the window, calling him.

"It's okay, baby," he called, starting to run after her, though he didn't know why. He wanted her away from him. "Daddy's okay," he called, though not loudly enough. He didn't feel like he could get a good breath.

"Daddy's okay," he called again, as the bus rounded the corner and went out of sight. He heard people yelling, but only vaguely, as he stumbled and started to fall.

He couldn't control his feet, and the ground started leaping toward him. When he hit it face first, he wondered why it didn't hurt.

CHAPTER

THREE

It had sounded like a .22, Maggie thought.

She pushed open the screen door and stepped out onto the crushed oyster shells that made up Lynn's parking lot. She squinted as she looked across 98, as though she might be able to see something, but there was nothing to see and she hadn't really expected there to be; the shot had sounded like it was at least a few blocks back.

"Could it have been a backfire?" one of the guys asked behind her.

Maggie shook her head distractedly. "No. Why don't you go on back inside, okay?"

"Okay. You want me to call 911?"

"It could just be somebody shooting at a possum or something," Maggie said without turning around. "But, yeah, go ahead and call the Sheriff's. But not 911 yet."

Maggie heard the screen door shut behind her, heard several people murmuring just inside the door. She pulled out her phone and dialed Dwight to see if he knew where the shot had come from, but he didn't answer.

She put the phone away, then jogged across 98 and up School Road, making good time despite the heaviness of her hiking boots. It had been a while since she'd worked out with any regularity. Lately, she got her only exercise from chasing suspects, working in her garden, or helping her daddy out on the oyster beds.

Although she wasn't necessarily in top shape, the weight in her chest and her elevated heart rate weren't due solely to the exertion. She could feel the wrongness of the moment; there was an almost palpable thickening of the air that portended something bad.

As Maggie rounded the corner, she saw a small group of people a bit more than halfway down the street, very close to the bus stop sign. They were in an approximation of a circle, and they were focused on someone on the ground. In one instant, she saw that Dwight wasn't among them. In the next, she recognized the soles of Dwight's new dress shoes, the legs of his uniform pants, and she sprinted.

"Dwight!" she screamed without meaning to. The people in the small crowd jerked their heads toward her. They were a blur of unrecognized faces, the only thing that registered in Maggie's brain was that they all looked vaguely horrified. "Dwight!" Maggie screamed again, her voice cracking.

Maggie should have been approaching cautiously. She should have been looking for someone with a firearm, even someone standing there in the little crowd, but she didn't. After sixteen years in law enforcement, her personal instincts overwhelmed her professional ones, and she skidded into the group, already on her knees by the time she reached Dwight.

He was on his stomach in the gravel, his face turned toward the street. His eyes were closed. There was a dark pool of blood spreading outward from underneath him, meandering slowly toward the side of the road.

Behind her, a man's voice said that he'd called 911. As Maggie turned Dwight over, a woman's voice above her said that they hadn't known whether to touch him. Two other people said simultaneously that he'd been shot. Maggie's brain registered the 911 call, then moved on.

Dwight's face was frighteningly pale, but Maggie saw his Adam's apple, the one everyone teased him about, move up and down as she turned him onto his back. His shirt and the front of his dress trousers were covered in blood. They were sopping with it.

There was grass and a scuff mark on his carefully polished belt. Five minutes ago, she thought without intending to, she had carefully picked a shrimp leg from his neatly-pressed uniform.

"Dwight!" Maggie ripped open his shirt. The white t-shirt underneath was soaked through. There was a small entrance wound just above his navel. It looked to be from a small caliber handgun. The amount of blood issuing from it terrified her, and she subconsciously asked God not to let it be an artery.

She looked up, her head swiveling from one onlooker to another, looking for something to help staunch the blood, but there was nothing. She ripped her t-shirt over her head and balled it up, pressed it down onto Dwight's wound with her right hand, and felt his neck for a pulse with her left. There was one, but it was weak.

Maggie heard sirens close-by. The Sheriff's Office was just over four miles away. She looked up. "What happened?" she asked the first face she saw, a short, gray-haired man in shorts and a t-shirt.

"I didn't see it, I just heard it," he said, eyes wide.

"It was some high school boys," said a woman's voice. Maggie turned to see a red-haired woman that she knew she knew, but she couldn't place her name. "Adrian Nichols and that boy...Stuart. Stuart Newman, Lyle Newman's oldest. Some other kids I don't know the names of."

"Why?" Maggie blurted, but she didn't wait for the answer. She leaned over Dwight, felt his blood, warm and slick, on her stomach as she put her face right over his. "Dwight, I'm here. I'm here."

"It was an accident," a young male voice said. Maggie glanced up at a tall, thin boy with dirty-blond hair and the beginnings of a goatee. "It was an accident," he repeated more quietly.

"Who?" Maggie barked the question at him.

"Ryan. Ryan Warner."

Maggie knew the name, but she didn't know why. It failed to conjure a face. She put a hand to the side of Dwight's face. "It's gonna be okay, I promise," she said.

The fact that Dwight had been meeting the bus suddenly asserted itself in her mind, and she jerked her head back up. "Where's his little girl?"

The red-headed woman answered, waving vaguely at the corner. "The bus left. With all the kids. He told the bus driver to go."

"She didn't get off the bus?"

"The elementary kids hadn't got off yet," the boy said. "Ma'am?"

Maggie looked up to see a tall, attractive brunette in her late forties or so. She was holding out a faded denim shirt. Maggie took it. "Thank you." She pressed it on top of her already soaked t-shirt before she realized that the woman had probably meant it for her to wear. She didn't care. She looked down at Dwight's face, which was even paler than it had been a moment earlier, just as his eyes fluttered open.

"Mag—," he started, his voice barely a whisper.

"I'm here, Dwight!" Maggie cried. "They're coming. Everybody's coming!"

He blinked a few times, but his eyes were unfocused and aimed somewhere over her shoulder. "I can't feel myself, Maggie."

"That's okay! It's okay!" Maggie said, but his eyes had fluttered closed again. "Dwight?"

Maggie checked his pulse. It was still there, but weaker. Maggie looked up as she heard a scream. She knew it as a woman's scream, but it sounded like a fierce, badly-wounded animal. Maggie looked up to see Dwight's wife Amy running across the street.

"Dwight!" she screamed, as her eyes lighted on her husband.

She was barefoot, and her pretty, flowered dress wrapped around her legs as she ran without thought or moderation. The left side of her red hair was curled, the right still straight.

The sirens sounded shrilly behind Maggie, along with a screeching of brakes and tires. She looked over her shoulder to see an EMT truck sandwiched between two SO cruisers.

Amy reached Maggie and Dwight, and she fell beside her husband, bits of gravel embedding themselves in her pale, freckled knees. "Baby? Dwight?"

Maggie put a hand on her arm as she heard the paramedics running behind her. "He's alive," she said, though she wasn't positive that was still true. "They're gonna help him, Amy."

Amy didn't take her eyes off her husband. She had a hand on either side of his face. "Dwight? Listen to me. Dwight?"

Larry Mancuso, one of the paramedics, dropped to his knees, his duffel beside him. Maggie had gone to school with his older brother, Jason. "Gunshot?" he asked without looking at her. Tate Moran, several years younger, ran up behind him with a gurney.

"Maybe six, seven minutes ago," Maggie answered. "It sounded like a .22."

"He's gonna be okay!" Amy said. She had streaks of mascara running down her cheeks. Maggie had never seen in her in make-up, except for Maggie and Wyatt's wedding. Today was a special day.

"Amy, I know you want to stay right by Dwight," Larry said as he pulled surgical dressings and a blood pressure cuff from his bag. "But I need you to let me have him, okay? I need some room."

"Amy," Maggie said quietly, as she put a hand to her underarm and lifted her. "You know Larry and Tate. They're the best, the very best."

Once standing, Amy looked at Maggie and smoothed her messy hair with a shaking hand. Her engagement ring glittered in what little sunlight there was. A tiny diamond. Maggie had helped Dwight pick it out. He'd had $185 to his name that day.

"Where are the kids?" Maggie asked her.

It took a moment for Amy to answer, her eyes fixed on the EMTs, and what they were doing to her husband. She looked up at Maggie suddenly, like her hearing had been delayed.

"They're with Tina," she answered quietly. "Next door."

Maggie nodded. She heard more cars screech to a stop behind her, but she didn't look. She stood next to Amy as they both watched Larry and Tate do their jobs. A moment later, she felt someone beside her. It was Wyatt, holding out his old gray flannel shirt, the one he kept in his truck for changing the oil or doing repairs..

He slipped it around her shoulders, and she took her eyes from the ground, watched his hands do up the buttons. There were only three buttons left on the shirt, but it was better than her standing there in her blood-stained bra. Wyatt's hands were steady, but when she looked up at his face, and his eyes met hers, she saw the fear. Beneath his impressive mustache, his mouth was set firmly, the lines around it no longer laughing.

Fewer than two minutes later, the EMTs loaded Dwight into the back of the van. Maggie had stepped forward, thinking she should go with him, but then real-ized it was Amy who needed to do that. It was Amy's place. Maggie watched her climb into the back of the van, and then it was gone, sirens wailing as it sped around the corner.

More deputies had arrived, as had Sheriff Bledsoe. He'd ordered several deputies to talk to the witnesses who were still standing there. Two other deputies moved their cruisers to block the road. Another had taped off the scene without Maggie noticing.

"Ryan Warner," she said to Wyatt.

"What?"

"Ryan Warner is the shooter."

"The kid from this morning?" he asked, his abundant brows meeting over his nose.

"What kid?" Maggie asked.

"On Sky's phone."

"I don't know," Maggie said, shaking her head. "I can't remember that kid's name."

"Stay here."

Maggie watched him walk over to Bledsoe and say a few words. Bledsoe turned and yelled for Myles Godfrey, a deputy with thick, black hair and thick black glasses. Wyatt walked back to Maggie as a light rain finally started to fall.

"Let's go," he said. "We'll take the truck."

He put a hand on Maggie's shoulder and turned her toward his truck. She looked over her shoulder at the ground where Dwight had just been.

Her t-shirt was stilled balled up, lying in the gravel now, unrecognizable as having ever been light blue. Dwight's blood was being diluted by the rain, and rivulets of it were disappearing into the gravel and grass. In a few minutes, it might even be gone. That just didn't seem right.

FOUR

ennett Boudreaux blinked a few raindrops from his long, dark lashes as he twisted another mango from one of the dwarf trees. It succumbed to his hand without protest, and he slipped it gently into the canvas tote on his shoulder.

The bit of sunlight still peeking through the clouds glinted on his hair, still full, and still mostly brown, with touches of silver at his ears. A damp lock of it fell over his forehead, and he brushed it back before turning to look at Miss Evangeline.

"Would you get back on the porch, please?" he asked, a bit of irritation in his voice. "It's starting to rain in earnest."

Miss Evangeline looked up sharply as she picked up a large mango from the ground. Her thick bi-focals were almost covered in raindrops, and her red bandana was doing nothing to keep her head dry. She tucked the mango into one of the cavernous pockets of her flowered house dress, the weight of it and three other mangoes threatening to pull the faded dress down around her feet. A Piggly-Wiggly bag hanging from the hook on her aluminum walker was laden with several more fallen fruits.

At close to one-hundred, if not beyond it, she weighed less than most first-graders. With her wrinkled, papyrus-like Creole skin and her scrawny frame, she often reminded him of a thin cigar.

"Why I got to go the porch, me?" she asked in her raspy voice. "You out here the rain."

Boudreaux watched her make preparations to straighten to her full fifty-seven inches. "Because I still have an immune system," he said. He turned back to the mango tree and reached for another ripe one. "Yours expired decades ago," he added quietly.

"What you say?" she barked behind him.

He turned to look at her. "I said I don't want you catching cold," he said more loudly.

Miss Evangeline's tongue rooted around her lower plate as she glared at him. "Boy, I been your nanny fifty-eight year," she snapped. "I don' need no short-pants Cajun boy try to baby me, no."

Boudreaux sighed, but tried to do it quietly. He was sixty-three years old, and while he was fit and could pass for a much-younger man, he certainly couldn't be confused with a boy in short pants.

"With all of these mango trees out here, you don't need to be getting yourself soaked picking up fallen fruit," he said.

His Low-Country style, two-story house was on a double lot that was rare in Apalach's Historic District. Aside from the garage and Miss Evangeline's small cottage, the entire back yard was given over to the nine full size and twelve dwarf mangoes that he had planted for her, mangoes that few people managed to grow this far north.

"I ain't gon' volunteer no more my mango that sorry squirrel, no," she said behind him. "Look here." She prodded at a mango with the toe of her terry-cloth house shoe. "One bite he take this one. One bite he take that one. Taste the mango then let it rot here the ground."

"We've got plenty."

"You got plenty money, too, but I don' see you throwin' it round the yard, no," she countered, slowly bending to fetch another mango. "Maybe you don' remember them day we don't have nothin'!"

"I remember, Miss Evangeline."

"Ain't gon' leave no mango for him, no," she went on, glaring at a mango in her hand. Half of it had been gnawed away. "I gon' clean up my shotgun. Blow his mangy ass right out his eye sockets, me, he come pillage me some more."

Boudreaux had confiscated her shotgun back in the eighties, but he didn't bother reminding her.

"Hey!"

Boudreaux looked up to see Amelia, his housekeep-er/cook and Miss Evangeline's daughter, standing at the top of the steps that led to the wraparound porch. Her skin was the same freckled shade as her mother's but she was tall, and her frame was solid and imposing.

"Oyster Radio say a sheriff deputy got shot," she called.

Boudreaux felt something slither in his stomach. "Who?"

"Don't say," she answered, the brisk breeze playing at the hem of her own faded house dress. "Got shot over to Eastpoint and on the way to the hospital."

Boudreaux pulled out his cell phone, thumbed open his recent calls list and pressed Maggie's number. It went to voice mail. He switched to his contacts list, raindrops tapping at his screen, until he found the number for the Sheriff's Office. He seldom called it; as the town's most-celebrated criminal, he had little occasion to do so. A woman answered.

"Maggie Redmond—Maggie Hamilton, please," he said.

"I'm sorry, she's not available," the woman said. He could hear tension and hurry in her voice. "Can someone else help you?"

"Where is she, please?" he asked, trying to sound more polite than his nerves urged him to be.

The woman didn't answer straightaway. "Who's calling, please?"

Boudreaux was accustomed to his name opening many doors, but this wasn't one of them. "Her father," he answered.

There was a moment's hesitation, then, "She's on her way to the hospital."

The voice went on, but Boudreaux had already lowered the phone and disconnected. He shoved it into his pocket, then hurried the several yards to the steps. He took them two at a time and dropped the bag of mangoes at Amelia's feet as he passed.

"I'll be back."

⚓   ⚓   ⚓

The emergency room at Weems Memorial was small but well equipped for most trauma cases. Dr. Stan Ridgeway had been the surgeon on call when the hospital was advised that Dwight was on the way, and he was there within a few minutes of Dwight's arrival.

The first order of business was to repair the common iliac artery, which had indeed been nicked by the bullet. As Dr. Ridgeway had quickly advised Amy, Maggie, Wyatt, and several members of Dwight's close-knit family, Dwight had lost a great deal of blood, which caused his blood pressure to drop far too low for extensive surgery. The plan was to repair the artery and give him the blood he needed, then airlift him to Port St.

Joe for the surgery to remove the bullet and repair the other damage it had caused. So far, they didn't know what that damage was.

Maggie and Wyatt leaned against the wall in the surgical waiting room, while Amy, along with Dwight's parents, waited around the corner, just outside the operating room. Maggie had seen the horror in Mrs. Shultz's eyes when she'd looked at Maggie's stomach, at her son's blood smeared there, and Maggie had hurried, with trembling fingers, to tie the tails of the shirt in a knot.

There was a window just a few feet away, with a vending machine on one side and a water dispenser on the other. The rain was pelting the glass, and Maggie tried to let the drum-like rhythm calm her mind.

Wyatt leaned against the wall beside her, making her feel stronger and calmer just by being present. He was lost in his own thoughts, she knew. It had been Wyatt who had hired Dwight, and before he'd resigned as sheriff, it had been Wyatt who had suggested he go for a promotion.

Wyatt cared deeply about all his people, and they were still *his* people, but Maggie knew he felt particularly protective of Dwight. She wished he wasn't trying to blame himself right now, but she knew that he was. As was she.

She reached over and wrapped a few of her fingers around a few of his. He rubbed them with his thumb as stared at the floor. Footfalls from around the corner made both of them turn their heads as Sheriff Bledsoe rounded the corner and hurried toward them. He was neat as a pin, as always, every remaining blond hair in place, his expensive tie and more moderate suit meant to make him more imposing than his small stature did. He carried a manila file folder in one hand.

"How is he?" he asked them while he was still a few yards away.

"They're repairing a nicked artery, so they can transport him to Sacred Heart," Wyatt said quietly.

Bledsoe stopped in front of them, his chest heaving just a bit, and looked from Wyatt to Maggie.

"We're interviewing everyone that was there, including the school bus driver, the neighbors that saw or heard it, the kids," he said. "Except for Dwight's kid. We haven't been able to locate this boy Ryan Warner yet."

"What about the other boys that were there? The ones that started the fight or whatever?" Maggie asked.

"I don't know why they bothered running," he answered. "They were all at home, except for the kid that stayed on scene. We're taking statements now."

"What happened?" Wyatt asked.

"Well, we have to compare stories, get everything filled in," Bledsoe answered. "But it appears that this kid Warner felt threatened by the other boys and pulled a gun. Dwight tried to intervene, to calm the situation, and from what we've heard so far, the shooting was accidental."

"But the kid had a gun," Maggie said. "On the school bus, and I assume at school beforehand. He took a gun to school."

"Yeah," Bledsoe said. "But the witnesses are saying the shooting wasn't intentional; Dwight was just in the wrong place at the wrong time."

"He shouldn't have been there," Maggie said. "He shouldn't be *here*. He should be at his promotion ceremony."

"He was," Bledsoe said. "Didn't he get to tell you?"

"What?"

"Yeah, this morning. We—"

"No, we were on our way there," Maggie insisted, wondering if he'd fallen on his head.

"Yeah, uh, I guess he forgot to tell you," Bledsoe said. "So, yeah. Sergeant's pay and sergeant's benefits as of eight this morning." He looked at Wyatt, who was staring at him, eyes narrowed. "Wyatt was there."

"It was nice," Wyatt said after a second.

Bledsoe held out the file folder. "I forgot to get you to sign as witness, though."

Maggie stared first at Bledsoe, who handed Wyatt his pen, and then at Wyatt, who used the wall as a desk to add his signature to the promotion documentation.

"Where's Dwight's wife? His family?" Bledsoe asked her.

It took Maggie a moment to answer, she was that taken aback by what he was telling them. "They're in the hall outside the operating room," she answered. "Down there."

Bledsoe took the folder and pen back from Wyatt. "I'll go speak with them. We'll need a statement from you, Lieutenant, but it can wait until you come in in the morning. Team meeting at 7:30."

He headed down the hall, and Maggie looked at Wyatt.

"Did he just do something really good?"

"Yeah," said Wyatt, who disliked him a little more than everyone else did, except perhaps for Maggie. "We can hate him for that later."

⚓   ⚓   ⚓

Bennett Boudreaux opened the glass door that led to the reception area for the ER. His hand-tailored, blue silk shirt was sodden, his expensive loafers and the hems of his tan trousers darkened by the rain.

The middle-aged woman at the reception desk looked up sharply as the door slammed shut. She watched as Boudreaux stalked up to her.

"Maggie Redmond, where is she?" he asked quickly.

"I don't know—"

"The sheriff's officer that was shot, where is the officer?" he asked more loudly. An old man with a portable oxygen tank and a bloody bandage on his knee looked over at him.

"In surgery," she answered, flustered at his tone. "But you'll have to wait—"

Boudreaux started for the swinging door that led to the belly of the ER.

"Mr. Boudreaux! You can't go back there!" she said, starting to rise. He stopped and turned, held up a finger.

"Don't," he said. His voice was soft, but his aquamarine eyes were not. "Don't get up from your desk."

She stared at the door as it swung shut behind him.

⚓   ⚓   ⚓

Wyatt had gone down the hall to the men's room. When Maggie heard hurried footsteps, she looked up, expecting him back, but it wasn't Wyatt, it was Bennett Boudreaux.

Maggie could count on one hand the number of times she had seen Boudreaux look less than perfect, and they had all been during a hurricane. As she pushed herself away from the wall, he saw her there and stopped for a moment, still several yards away.

He blinked a couple of times, then sighed. His clothes were wet, his hair wet as well, and he had obviously run his hands through it to push it back, like he tended to do. It made him look like an older James Dean. An older James Dean who had left himself out in the rain.

Maggie stood there and waited for him as he came toward her. Every time she saw him, she was glad and every time she saw him, she was conflicted. First he was her friend, however inadvisable that might have been.

Then she found out he was her biological father. Sometimes she liked that and sometimes she just missed her friend.

Their friendship hadn't lost its intimacy or its fascination, but of course it couldn't be exactly the same, either. At least, now that everyone, especially Wyatt, knew that he was her father, some of the tension over their relationship had eased.

"Maggie," he said when he reached her.

"Mr. Boudreaux." She brushed a bang out of her eye. "Why are you here?"

"I heard that an officer was shot, and was told you were on your way here," he answered quietly.

He blinked again, and Maggie thought his eyes had watered just a bit.

"It's Dwight Shultz," she said. She knew Boudreaux knew Dwight—knew his whole family. Every fisherman, oysterman and shrimper sold his catch to Boudreaux's wholesale seafood business. He wasn't the only game in town, but he was the biggest and, having come from poor oystering stock in Louisiana, he made a point of paying more than anyone else.

"I see. Is he alive?"

Maggie swallowed, and made herself lift her chin. "So far. Yes."

He stepped back, let out a slow breath, and leaned against the vending machine.

"What happened?"

Maggie shook her head. "I don't really know. We were having lunch at Lynn's. He went to get his little girl from the school bus, and apparently he tried to break up a fight. Kids. It was a kid—a teenager—that shot him."

"Do your parents know?" he asked. "It's on the radio. If they hear about it…"

"They're in the Keys with my aunt and uncle. I left Daddy a voice mail, though."

He nodded, and they were silent for a few moments. His blue eyes, as always, seemed to pin her to thin air. He stepped over to the water dispenser, pulled a folded, white handkerchief from his pants pocket, and wet it slightly. Then he came back to her and gently wiped at her neck. When he pulled the cloth away, it was smeared with red.

He folded it over, then wiped at the side of her face, near her ear.

"I was afraid," he said quietly.

"Me, too."

"Hey," Maggie heard from a few feet away. She and Boudreaux both looked up to see Wyatt standing there, his hands on his hips. He was frowning at them.

As Sheriff, Wyatt had been professionally disdainful of Bennett Boudreaux. As Maggie's best friend and eventual fiancé, the dislike had been much more personal. Aside from the fact that a friendship between a cop and a known criminal was never a good idea, Wyatt had been convinced that Boudreaux was actually in love with Maggie.

Learning that Boudreaux was Maggie's biological father alleviated that concern, but it didn't do much to change Wyatt's view of the man. As for Boudreaux, he actually liked Wyatt, if somewhat grudgingly.

"Amy just texted me," Wyatt said. "The surgeon's coming out to talk to them in just a minute. She says to come on back there."

Maggie's heartbeat quickened. "Okay."

She looked at Boudreaux, who was folding the handkerchief again.

"I'll be praying for Dwight," he said quietly. "I've known the Shultz men a long time; they do what they have to do. Dwight needs to take care of his family."

Maggie nodded. "Thank you for coming over here."

Boudreaux nodded. "I'll just go rinse this out."

"Wait." Maggie stared at the bloody cloth. "Don't. I'll wash it."

Boudreaux stared at her a moment, and she could see in his eyes that he understood.

"Thank you." He handed her the handkerchief. "No hurry. It was good to see you, Maggie."

"It was good to see you, too."

He nodded at Wyatt as he started away. "Wyatt."

"Dad."

There was a twitch of a smile at the edge of Boudreaux's mouth as he walked away.

CHAPTER
FIVE

Dwight had been made as stable as the surgeon had time to make him; he'd been given blood and was still receiving it. The damage to the artery had been hastily repaired. Dwight's blood pressure was higher, but not as high as it needed to be. Nonetheless, there was nothing further that could be done for him at Weems Memorial, and the helicopter from Sacred Heart was on its way. It would pick up Dwight, and Amy, in the back parking lot.

When asked repeatedly by Amy, Dr. Ridgeway relented enough to say that the best things that could have been for Dwight at Weems, had been. No one asked for any percentages or predictions, and while no one's heart was broken, no one's heart was lightened, either.

Maggie and Wyatt left by the front entrance in order to stay out of the way of the Medi-Vac. When they did, they found that the rain had slowed to a drizzle, but the wind had picked up a bit.

Just across the parking lot was a circle of about twenty people, heads bowed and hands joined. There were a couple of off-duty deputies and Apalach PD officers among them. Everyone on duty was out looking for Ryan Warner.

Maggie stopped just outside the entrance and stared at the gathering, about twenty yards away beneath a live oak.

Wyatt grabbed her hand and tugged her along beside him. When they reached the circle, a lady that worked at the Marathon station and James Francis from Apalach PD created an opening for them.

Maggie bowed her head, and listened as a nearby Sabal palm swished in the breeze and a helicopter lifted its cargo into the sky.

⚓   ⚓   ⚓

The kids took the news about Dwight very hard. Maggie had forgotten that school had let out early, and she'd been unprepared for telling them so soon. Wyatt had texted both of them as soon as he and Maggie had gotten to the hospital, but he'd shared no details, only telling them that he and Maggie were okay.

After both she and Wyatt had done what they could to reassure and comfort the kids, Maggie left them each to their own individual means of dealing with the shooting, while she went to take a much-needed shower.

It was only when she watched small rivers of blood run down her legs, and the pink-tinted lather rushing toward the drain, that she finally started feeling the physical and emotional effects of the day. She was suddenly terribly weary, and her eyes stung, then loosed warm tears, as she leaned against the tiled shower wall.

She stayed there for some time, letting the hot water soothe her. Outside the bathroom, Stoopid tapped repeatedly at the door.

Several hours later, Dwight's father called to give them an update. As most .22 bullets do, this one had banged around inside Dwight before deciding to lodge between the L4 and L5 vertebrae. Before they could address the bullet, repairs had to be made to Dwight's large intestine and pancreas, and the hasty surgery on the iliac artery improved upon. According to the surgeon who had operated on Dwight, the major concerns at this point were infection caused by the breach of the large intestine, and damage to the spinal cord.

It was possible that removing the large hematoma near the spine would relieve pressure on the spinal cord and Dwight would be fine. It was equally possible that the bullet itself had done enough damage to render Dwight paralyzed.

First, Dwight's system needed to strengthen enough to undergo what would be a risky and probably lengthy surgery. He would remain in the ICU at Sacred Heart through the next forty-eight hours, and if all went well, they were hoping to be able to take him back into surgery on Monday.

No one offered the Shultz family any predictions. Until the team of a neurosurgeon and an orthopedic surgeon were able to open him back up, it was really anybody's guess.

Wyatt had been getting calls throughout the rest of the day and the evening, updates from those who were working on the case. Who had been interviewed, who had not. Tips and suggestions regarding the location of Ryan Warner, none of which had panned out thus far.

At first, Maggie had bristled at the fact that everybody was calling Wyatt and not her, though people had reported to Wyatt for over ten years, and some still called him "Boss," Dwight included. Also, Wyatt quietly pointed out that they would have given Dwight the same break if it had been Maggie who had been shot. She immediately knew the truth of that and mentally backhanded herself for thinking about her own feelings or need for control.

Later that night, after the kids had retired to their rooms, Maggie walked out the back door and headed for the dock. Stoopid and Coco tapped and jangled behind her, past the firepit, the garden, and the chicken run. Maggie could hear the girls gossiping inside the coop.

She was surrounded by the sounds that soothed her. The rustling of the palm fronds in the last of the storm-birthed breeze. The soft thumps of her bare feet on the worn planks of the dock. The gentle lap of the water against the pilings.

She sat down at the end of the dock, letting her legs hang over the edge. Stoopid fidgeted on one side of her commenting on the weather. Coco leaned against her shoulder on the other side, the way she did when she knew someone needed a hug.

After a while, Maggie heard footsteps behind her on the dock. She knew they were Wyatt's; no one else was big enough to make that much noise without shoes. He sat down behind her, one leg on either side of her, and his arms wrapped gently around her. She put her hands on his and held them there.

"Amy called," he said after a moment. "No real change, but he's still with us. She wanted you to know. She also said to tell you 'Thank you.'"

Maggie let out a soft snort without meaning to. "Thank you," she repeated softly.

"Ah, I see," Wyatt said quietly. "It's your fault."

"I know it's not my fault. I just wish…" She shrugged. "I don't know. I wish something."

Wyatt sighed, and kissed the top of her head. "We don't wish. We deal with what we've got."

It took Maggie a moment to answer. "Yeah."

Maggie laid awake long into the night, Wyatt snoring softly beside her, his arm draped over her chest. At the foot of the bed, Coco was draped across her feet, snoring a little more loudly. Coco had been sleeping with her since she was a puppy. Since the wedding, it had become her habit to sneak onto the bed once Wyatt was asleep. It had become Wyatt's habit to wake up in the morning and pretend he was surprised.

Maggie had tried deep breathing, and counting oyster skiffs or chickens, but she'd been unable to shut her brain down long enough to fall asleep. She couldn't stop thinking about the fact that Sky had been at school that morning, that an armed and angry boy had walked down the same halls, maybe even passed Sky at some point during the day.

Several times, Maggie's mind threw up a picture of Sky studying at the library, wearing her earbuds as she always did, hunching over her books, ripe for surprise. When that picture wasn't terrorizing her, the names were. Columbine. Sandy Hook. More recently, and much closer to home, Stoneman-Douglas. These and other names she could remember repeated over and over in her head until she knew she needed to get up in order to quiet them.

She pulled her feet out from under Coco, and the dog raised her head to see what Maggie needed.

"Stay, baby," Maggie whispered, and rubbed at her silky ear before she swung her legs over the side of the bed and got up.

She quietly shut the door behind her, and walked down the dark hallway to the living room. Stoopid, who could hear anything unless someone was speaking to him, woke from his perch on the ceiling fan and stretched out his neck.

"Don't," Maggie said sharply.

He coughed back the crow he was working on, made a few preparatory flaps, then flew down to the floor and followed her into the kitchen.

The only light was from the moon that hung brightly over the bay. It seeped across the yard and through the blinds over the sliding glass door. Maggie opened the fridge and grabbed a water bottle. Stoopid mentioned the opportunity before her, and she grabbed a few leaves of lettuce and dropped them into his dish.

She leaned against the sink as she drank her water. It was sweet, and almost too cold. She stared past her reflection in the window to the dark beyond. After a moment, she could make out some dark shapes in the garden, and a few glints of moonlight on the water near the dock.

She finished her water, tripped over Stoopid, and went back down the hall. Not wanting to wake Wyatt by using their bathroom, she used the one in the hallway. As she washed her hands afterwards, she caught sight of her face in the mirror. Looking at herself had never been one of her favorite things, but now she looked weary and red-eyed and at least five years older than she had the morning before.

She looked away, dried her hands, and turned off the light on her way out. She was about to pass the door to Sky's room, but stopped, deliberated, and then eased the door open. Sky was on her side, facing the door, and Maggie stood there for a moment watching her, though she couldn't see her face. She was about to pull the door closed again when Sky spoke.

"What is it?' she asked quietly.

"Nothing," Maggie answered. "Just checking on you. I couldn't sleep."

Sky sat up, her bedlinens rustling. Now Maggie could just make out her face, silver in the moonlight. "Are you okay?"

Maggie nodded. "Yeah. It's just been a rough day."

"Have you heard anything else about Dwight?"

"No. Go back to sleep."

Maggie started, again, to go back out.

"Mom?"

"What?"

It took Sky a moment to answer, and when she did her voice was uncharacteristically gentle.

"It didn't happen."

"What didn't?" Maggie asked.

"I'm okay."

Maggie blinked a few times, her chest warming at her daughter's attempt to comfort *her*. Just a couple of years ago, two out of three conversations between them had ended with one or both of them sighing and walking away. That she could now hug Sky without her pulling away, that they could laugh together, or say "I love you," was a miracle freshly acknowledged at least once a week.

And now she was leaving. And if things had been different today, she wouldn't be here at all.

Maggie mentally shook herself, tired of her own morbidity and self-indulgence. She walked over to the bed, leaned over, and kissed Sky's temple. She drank in the familiar aromas of Herbal Essence, coconut lotion and sun-warmed skin, as Sky accepted her kiss.

Maggie straightened up. "You're still my Boo," she said. "I love you, Sky."

"I love you too, dude." She flopped onto her back, and her face disappeared into the shadows. "Now go away so I can get some sleep. My frontal lobe is still developing."

CHAPTER
SIX

Maggie sat at the long, oval table in the conference room and stared out the picture window over the far end of the table. Wyatt sat beside her, nursing his first mountainous Mountain Dew of the day. They had been at the hospital in Port St. Joe by six-thirty this morning. There had been no real change in Dwight's condition.

Amy's parents had been watching the kids at their home, as Amy stayed with Dwight. His parents were taking shifts accompanying her, and several other family members had taken vigils as well. Amy's sister and best friend were with her when Maggie and Wyatt arrived. They weren't allowed to see Dwight. There really was no purpose in them being there, except to show support.

Maggie had felt inadequate and insufficient and had apologized to Amy for not being able to stay with her.

Amy had brushed her tangled bangs from her eyes and propped a hand on her slim hip. "You're doing what I need you to do," she'd said.

It was now seven-thirty, and they were awaiting Sheriff Bledsoe's arrival. Around the table, were several deputies who had been assigned to the team investigating Dwight's shooting.

Essentially, everyone was on that team, including James Lyle, who normally headed up the narcotics team. Bledsoe had scheduled a skeleton crew to handle existing cases and patrol shifts and arranged for Apalach PD to take on anything new that wasn't a homicide or hostage situation. Meanwhile, seven other deputies were tasked solely with looking for Ryan Warner.

The door opened, and Bledsoe walked in, carrying a green file folder that matched the ones sitting in front of each person at the table.

"Good morning," he said quietly, shutting the door.

He was greeted, either verbally or non-verbally, by the people in the room, then took a seat at the head of the table.

"Okay. We've all had a blow. We all had a shock yesterday," he said. "Now it's time to see what we have to work with so far, and what we need to do from here."

He opened his folder, and everyone else followed suit. "Based on the initial statements from the witnesses, here's what we're dealing with. According to Ryan Warner's mother, Ginny, and one of the boys at the scene,

Brian Gentry—this is the kid that didn't run—Adrian Nichols, Stuart Newman, Drake Woods and this kid Brian have been harassing Ryan Warner all year."

Maggie looked at photographs of each of the boys as Bledsoe talked. Some were school pictures, some were clearly from phones or Facebook; Stuart and Adrian both had mug shots.

Bledsoe looked up from his file. "The kid's new, just moved here from Orlando over the summer. He's a little geeky, dorky, whatever, a real target." He looked back down. "Anyway, Thursday night, a video of Ryan Warner, with these boys in the background, popped up on a YouTube channel belonging to Nichols and Newman. Apparently, this little group of thugs accosted the kid in an empty classroom, and something about a mouse or a rat, and the kid wet himself a little. Enough to show on camera."

He looked around the table. "I'm sure it's no surprise that a bunch of kids shared this video on Facebook and Instagram and wherever, and basically, just about everybody at school saw it. No doubt, this included Warner, because he took his father's .22 to school yesterday morning."

"Any idea what his intentions were?" Wyatt asked.

"Not for certain, no," Bledsoe said. "I think only the kid knows. His mother swears he's a good kid, no violence ever. Of course, we hear that a lot, but he has no record of any kind, not even fighting in school."

"Where'd the father keep the gun?" James asked.

"Father's dead," Bledsoe answered. "T-boned coming off I-4 two years ago. The kid and his mother were in the car with him, minor injuries. The mother kept the gun loaded in her nightstand for protection, but she says the kid was scared of guns, never went near it."

"Well, now he did," James said, bitterness lacing his voice.

"Yeah. Anyway." Bledsoe cleared his throat. "These boys get off the bus yesterday and Nichols gets real aggressive and threatening with Ryan Warner. Dwight shows up to get his little girl. To bring her here for the promotion ceremony." He stopped to cough into his fist. "He gets there right about the time the kid pulls the gun and he tries to intervene. This snotbag Nichols thinks he's a big man, gonna save the day, and tosses a backpack at the kid while the kid's talking to Dwight. Gun goes off."

Bledsoe let out a breath and sat back in his leather chair. Maggie stared at Ryan Warner's senior picture, resenting the fact that he reminded her of Kyle, with his dark hair and gentle good looks. She didn't care; looks meant nothing. She looked up at Bledsoe.

"Why do Nichols and Newman have mug shots?"

Myles answered for his boss. "Nichols has two marks on his record. Back in Alabama, where he's from, he got caught keying a teacher's car. Then last summer he got in a fight with another kid at Bayfront Park. Newman was involved, too."

"I'm surprised we don't know this kid Nichols," Wyatt said.

"He's only been here since late 2016," Bledsoe answered. "Dad's a shrimper from Alabama."

"I know him," Myles said. "PD was busy that day; I'm the one took him in for the fight. Had to. He had a wrench, split the other kid's lip with it."

"Nice," Wyatt said. "So why has this little citizen been allowed to bully Warner all year?"

James spoke up. "The mother says she's been to the principal's office about it three times, but Beth Freeman said her hands were tied. No witnesses to any of the bullying involving Ryan Warner. She can't take disciplinary action unless another student or adult is a witness."

"Well, that's crap," Wyatt said. "When I was a kid, you could get suspended for smelling like cigarette smoke. You didn't even have to get caught smoking."

"Welcome to today," James said.

"Okay, let's talk about the tasks at hand for today," Bledsoe said, flipping some pages in his file. "Obviously, we need to locate Warner, and we've got every officer on duty searching. As far as the people at this table, we need to interview or re-interview key people, and I want to switch up, get second perspectives on every statement, so everybody's trading witnesses. Myles and Hammond, I want you to do the second interview with the bus driver, this guy Frank Walters that lives on School Road, and Adrian Nichols and his parents. James and Quincy, talk to the principal, this list of contacts from Orlando that Myles got from Ryan's mother, and the other two kids in this little gang."

"What about Ryan's cell phone?" Maggie asked. "I assume he has one. Have we tried to ping it?"

Quincy spoke up. "It's off. Like, the battery's out. The last location we have is for the woods out past Grainger, something like seven minutes after he ran. He pinged off the tower back there."

That was the street toward the back of Ryan and Dwight's neighborhood.

"Probably how he thought to turn it off," Myles said. "He saw the tower."

Bledsoe turned a page, took a sip of water from the glass in front of him, and went on. "PJ and Yarrow, you're in charge of re-canvassing the neighborhood around School Road. Let's see if anyone saw Ryan after the shooting that we didn't talk to yesterday. Or anyone who's seen him since then without knowing it was important."

"Got it," Greg Yarrow said, rubbing at the bridge of his nose.

Bledsoe looked over at Wyatt. "You're here because we don't have her," he said, nodding at Maggie. "You—"

"What do you mean we don't have me? I'm sitting right here," Maggie said.

"You're sitting here as a courtesy, because Dwight is your partner," Bledsoe said shortly. "I don't want you anywhere near this."

"Why?"

"What do you mean, why? Because Dwight is your partner. You're understandably upset."

"We're *all* upset," James interjected.

"Yeah, but we weren't all there while Dwight was bleeding on the ground," Bledsoe answered, not unkindly.

Maggie felt her blood rushing to her head, felt the heat flooding her face. She opened her mouth, determined to keep her tone non-confrontational, but Wyatt stuck up his palms before she could speak.

"With all due respect," he said, "She's going to work the case whether she has permission or not."

"I don't like threats, Wyatt—"

"It's not a threat. It's the voice of experience," Wyatt responded calmly. "She'd do it if I was still sitting in that chair. She *has* done it."

"That doesn't make it a good idea."

"Look, you're in charge. But we need all hands on deck here, don't you think?"

Bledsoe sighed, looked from Maggie to Wyatt. "All right, look. You work together today, okay? We'll play it by ear from there."

"Thank you," Maggie said.

"You guys have Ryan's mother, the two ladies that live across the street from the scene, and the kid's science teacher. Names are on your notes, Wyatt."

"That won't take very long," Maggie said.

"No. but I'm hoping we have Ryan Warner in custody by the time all of you get done with your interviews," Bledsoe answered. "Tasks for this afternoon, the rest of the day, that'll depend on whether we have him or not."

There was a quick rap on the door and Deputy Mike Wear opened it with a jerk without waiting for an answer. "We got a problem," he said to Bledsoe.

"What?"

"Dwight's shooting," Mike answered. "It's on Facebook."

"What the hell?" James barked, getting up.

"*What?*" Bledsoe yelled, standing. "Where? Let me see it!"

Mike stepped over to the table, phone in hand. "My kid, Jason, sent it to me. I've got it pulled up. We've also had six phone calls about it in the last five minutes."

Everyone but Maggie gathered around Mike. Maggie walked quickly out of the room and leaned up against the wall as the door swung shut.

Less than a minute later, Wyatt opened the door. Maggie heard raised voices behind him. His deeply-tanned face had a sickly tone.

"It's over, come back in," he said shortly, and held the door for her. She went back into the conference room.

"What do we need to do to get that crap off the internet?" Bledsoe was barking.

Myles spoke up. He was visibly shaken. "Fastest way is to get the kids to take it down. But I think we need to get with the FBI in case they refuse."

"I don't care if we have to blow up the internet," Wyatt said, his jaw tight. "We need to get it down before Amy or his family sees it, if they haven't already."

"Refuse? No, hell no they won't refuse!" Bledsoe said. "Myles, you and Hammond split up, one to Newman's and one to Nichols'. Get it down." He pointed at Mike. "Go call the DA, find out what we can charge these punks with. Obstruction, something."

As Myles, Hammond and Mike started out of the room, Bledsoe looked at everyone remaining.

"Sometimes I'm glad I don't have kids. Go."

As Maggie and Wyatt walked down the hall toward the front door, they passed one deputy or staffer after another who looked like they'd been pole-axed.

"Okay, we're working together, but we split up. It'll be faster," Wyatt said once they were out the door. He held up his copy of the file folder. "I'll take these DeMott, DeWitt, DeWhatever ladies on School Road. You take the mother. You'll be good with her. Then we meet up."

Maggie was working hard to keep up with his pace. They were parked next to each other, and they both stopped when they reached her Jeep. Wyatt opened the door for her, but he was looking at the hood. He hadn't met her eye since he'd watched the video.

Maggie looked up at him. "Was it bad?" It was a stupid question, but she knew he knew what she meant, even if she couldn't phrase it right.

He didn't look at her right away. She saw his jaw tighten, saw his temple throb. He draped an arm on the top of her door, sighed, and finally looked at her. He hadn't looked that sad since her ex-husband had been blown up right in front of them.

"You don't need to see it," he said. "Nobody did."

CHAPTER

SEVEN

Ryan and his mother, Ginny, lived in a small but neat cottage just a few blocks up from School Road. Maggie took the long way to get there, not yet ready to pass the bus stop.

She had called ahead, and a small voice on the other end had told her that she'd taken the day off and would be waiting for Maggie. Maggie pulled into the gravel driveway and parked behind a dark green, ten-year-old Saturn sedan.

The front yard was small but had been recently mowed. Maggie wondered if Ryan Warner had done it. Next to the front steps, on either side of a path that was missing several pavers, were two hibiscus bushes, one coral, and the other red. There was one tree in the front yard, a small Palmetto, and there were bunches of impatiens in various colors planted beneath it.

The house needed new gutters and downspouts, it could stand to be painted, and the front steps were listing just slightly to starboard, but someone was trying to make the place a home.

Maggie was halfway up the walk, her hiking boots thumping dully on the stone pavers, when the front door opened.

Ginny Warner looked to be a few years younger than Maggie. It was hard to tell for sure, with the woman's blond hair shoved messily into a ponytail, her face devoid of makeup, and dark smears of sleeplessness beneath her eyes.

"Mrs. Warner?" Maggie asked, as she reached the top step.

The woman nodded, then lowered her eyes and stepped back. She opened the door a bit wider, and Maggie walked past her into a short entryway. To the left, an archway opened into a small living room. To the right, a matching arch led to a dining room. Maggie could see notebooks and papers spread around the solid oak table, a coffee mug in the middle of them.

Maggie looked at Ginny Warner as the woman shut the door quietly. "I'm Maggie Hamilton," she said to be polite. "Where would you like to talk?"

Mrs. Warner looked around, like she was unfamiliar with the house, then held a hand out toward the dining room. "I'm in here," she said.

As Maggie followed her into the room, she glanced at several pictures hanging on the wall on either side of the arch. In one, a pre-adolescent Ryan posed with his parents beneath a Christmas tree. Mrs. Warner looked twenty years younger, and Ryan looked happy. He hadn't looked happy in his senior picture.

Ginny Warner pulled out the chair at the end of the table, in front of the papers and books, and Maggie sat to her right. She could just see into a kitchen with freshly painted gray walls. She could hear the refrigerator humming. The only other sound was the ticking of the clock over the bricked-up fireplace.

The other woman coughed quietly and wrapped her hands around her mug. "I was just…uh, trying to find…I was looking through his notebooks and stuff, trying to find some hint or sign that he was going to… do what he did."

"May I call you Ginny?" Maggie asked, pulling her notepad and pen from her purse. The woman nodded. "Ginny, did your son say anything to you Thursday night about this video that was uploaded, or about the incident in the classroom?"

Ginny looked at her, then quickly looked away. Her eyes were pointed at the front window, but the curtains were pulled tightly closed. Maggie wondered if people had been walking or driving by, trying to see what a possible killer's house looked like.

"Maybe he would have," Ginny finally answered. She looked back at Maggie. "If I had been home." She lifted the mug but put it back down without drinking. "I work two jobs. I've had to, since my husband died. We lost our house in Orlando, even though I was making decent money."

Maggie nodded. "So, you were working Thursday night?"

"Yes. I work at the BP four nights a week. More if I can get the hours."

"What time did you go in?"

"I went straight from my day job," Ginny answered. "During the week, I work days at Century-21."

"Are you a real estate agent?"

"No. Maybe one of these days, if I can take the class. Right now I'm the administrative assistant."

"Okay." Maggie made a note, then looked up again. "What time did you get home Thursday?"

"Just after twelve."

"So, did you see Ryan at all Thursday?"

"Just in the morning, before he went to school," Ginny answered. "We were talking about what he needed to take with him when he leaves for UCF. He has a full scholarship."

Her face suddenly seemed to fold in on itself, and she put a hand over her mouth, though she didn't make a sound. Maggie waited.

After a moment, Ginny lowered her hand and swallowed hard before continuing. "He worked so hard for that scholarship."

Maggie and Ryan's mother both knew he wouldn't be getting a chance to use it. Even if the shooting was an accident, he had committed a felony by taking the gun to school. At best, if Dwight survived, he would be charged with especially aggravated assault on a law enforcement officer. If Dwight didn't survive, she doubted any local DA or judge would let him plead involuntary manslaughter. She didn't even know if that option existed.

"What about yesterday morning, Ginny? Did you see Ryan then?"

"No. Mornings after I work at the second job, I sleep in until eight. His bus is at seven."

"Okay. Did he text you or call you during the morning? Before the shooting?"

Ginny shook her head. "No. He isn't supposed to call me at work unless it's an emergency or my lunch hour. They don't like us to get personal calls."

Maggie nodded. "So you haven't seen your son since Thursday morning?"

Maggie's tone was gentle, but she saw the defensiveness immediately.

"I have to work these hours," Ryan's mother said, her voice raised and breaking. "I didn't want Ryan to get a job; he has to focus on his schoolwork."

"Ma'am, I was a single mother for several years. I understand what it takes to try to keep everything together," Maggie said. "I've had many days where I didn't see my kids awake."

Ginny swallowed, rubbing nervously at her coffee mug. "How old are your kids?"

"My son's turning thirteen. My daughter is seventeen."

She saw the other woman's eyes flicker. "Does she go to Franklin?"

"Yes. She's a senior, too."

"What's her name?" Ginny asked, then shook her head. "I'm sorry, I shouldn't be asking you that. I just wondered if Ryan knew her."

"He did," Maggie said simply. "She was his peer-to-peer mentor the first week of school." Ginny shook her head slightly, confused. "It's something they do for new students. The mentor shows them where their classes are, introduces them around, answers questions. That kind of thing."

The other woman looked at Maggie for a long time. She seemed to be appraising her, but not unkindly. "You must hate Ryan."

"Why do you say that? Because he shot a fellow officer?"

"Well, that, yes. But I meant because he took a gun to your daughter's school."

Maggie took a moment to answer. There was some truth to what Ginny Warner was saying, but Maggie was asking for her help to locate her son, and that help wouldn't be forthcoming if the boy's mother was afraid of her.

"Ginny, obviously I don't condone what Ryan did, taking the gun to school," she said carefully. "I don't know what his intentions were, but he didn't use it on school property. Maybe he meant to—"

"He wouldn't have!"

"Maybe not. We don't know. But he didn't." Maggie chose her words with care. "My job is to protect the people who live in this county. Your son is one of those people, even though Dwight Shultz is my friend. The most important thing, at this point, is to find your son safe, bring him in safely, and hear his side of this story."

Maggie wasn't sure how accurate it was, but she hoped it sounded sincere.

Ginny Warner thought for a moment, then nodded.

Maggie tapped her pen against her open notepad. "Okay, what about what's been going on with Ryan at school? Can you tell me about that?"

"Ryan's been having problems with those other boys almost since school started," Ginny answered after a moment. "I don't know all of the kids' names, just Adrian Nichols and Stuart Newman."

"What kinds of problems?"

"At first, they just teased him, picked on him the way smaller boys or new kids get picked on, until the other kid gets bored. But then it got worse."

She stared down at one of her son's notebooks. Maggie followed her gaze. There was a small sketch of a dolphin on the cover, like he'd been doodling. It was good.

"They started bumping against him in the hallway," Ginny continued. "Slamming his locker shut when he was trying to get something out, things like that."

"Is that when you went to the principal's office?"

"No. Ryan asked me not to. He was embarrassed. I didn't ask for a conference until Adrian Nichols shoved Ryan when he was walking home from the bus stop. Ryan fell and scraped the side of his face on the sidewalk."

"What did the principal say?"

"That she couldn't do anything."

"But Ryan had a physical injury."

"It wasn't school property." She sighed. "Ms. Freeman was sympathetic, but she couldn't take any kind of disciplinary action."

"But you went in to speak to her again?" Maggie asked.

"Yes. In November, right before the Thanksgiving holiday."

"What for?"

"Stuart Newman tripped Ryan in the shower after gym," Ginny answered. "Adrian Nichols was there, too."

"Was Ryan hurt?"

"He was a little bruised. On his knee."

"What did Ms. Freeman do about that incident?"

Ginny sighed. "She seemed like she wanted to do something, but she couldn't. "

"But this was on school property," Maggie said.

"No witnesses. She did call them into her office, but it was Ryan's word against two other boys."

Maggie chewed at the corner of her lip. "There are cameras in the locker room, aren't there? Not in the shower, but somewhere. You'd be able to see that all three boys were in the shower room."

Ginny shook her head. "There's a camera over the coach's office and one over the door to the locker room, on the outside. The other two boys said Ryan slipped and fell on his way out of the shower."

Maggie sighed. "Okay, what about the third time you went in to the school?"

"There wasn't really another incident," Ginny answered. "At least, not where Ryan got hurt. I just—they were just relentless. Teasing, threatening, crowding him. He hated going to school."

She suddenly put her face in her hands and took a deep breath that Maggie could almost feel. After a moment, she put her hands down and straightened her shoulders. "I hated to send him. If I didn't work two jobs, and if he didn't have so much riding on his grades, I would have pulled him out and tried to homeschool him the rest of the year. You don't understand what it was like to make him go to school, knowing how scared he was sometimes, and how much he dreaded it. It's my job to protect him." She leaned forward, her eyes widening. "It's our job to *protect* our kids!"

Maggie nodded. "Yes."

Ryan's mother sat back against her chair and put her fingers up to her mouth, as though to silence herself. Maggie changed tacks.

"Tell me about how your son handled your husband's death. Was he angry? Did he act out?"

"Of course he was angry," Ginny answered calmly. "He didn't understand. We were hit by a drunk driver who'd had two DUIs and didn't have any insurance. We lost Paul, and then we lost everything else. We didn't have any life insurance. We'd been meaning to get some, but it just felt like we had so many other things to budget for, and we were young, you know?"

She took a sip of coffee that had to be ice cold.

"But no, he didn't act out," she said. "He was mostly just sad. Paul wasn't a buddy, or very affectionate. He was the son of an Army colonel, so he was kind of reserved, but he was a good man, and he was solid. He went to the graduations and the awards and the field days. He was there if Ryan needed advice."

Maggie asked a few more questions about Ryan's background, his relationships with other kids at Franklin, and his temperament. Then she changed topics. "Ginny, do you have any idea where Ryan could be right now?"

The woman shook her head slowly. "I don't. I drove around for hours yesterday, last night. Looking. I just didn't know where to go."

"Where did you look?"

"I went over to the island, because he likes it over there. Mostly the state park. I drove all around over there." She thought for a moment. "I went all around the neighborhood here, of course. To the school. I even went over to Apalach, because he likes the downtown. He spends a lot of time at the library, and at the bookstore, the one on Commerce Street."

"Downtown Books & Purl."

"Right, yes. I drove everywhere I could think of over there, but he just wasn't there."

Maggie wrapped things up a few minutes later, gave Ryan's mother her card with her cell phone number, and urged her to call if she heard from Ryan or if the boy came home. She tried to make her understand that the safest thing for her son was to be in custody.

She didn't mention that the safest thing for her son was to be without a gun. Not only because of his probable state of mind, but because every law enforcement officer in the county knew he was armed. None of the people she worked with wanted to harm a kid, not even a kid who had shot one of their own, but if Ryan Warner even looked like he was pulling out a gun, he was probably going to get hurt.

Ginny Warner led Maggie to the front door and opened it for her, but she reached out and put a hand on Maggie's arm as she passed. Maggie stopped and looked at her.

"I know you're a police officer, but you're also a mom," Ginny said. "Please. Please don't let Ryan get hurt. He didn't mean to hurt anyone. I know you can't know that, but I do. Believe another mother's heart. Please."

Maggie nodded, agreeing to nothing she couldn't guarantee, and eager to get away from Ginny Warner before she could see the odds reflected in Maggie's eyes.

EIGHT

The two women who opened the door to Wyatt were clearly sisters. They were both very pretty, and they had the same dark brown hair. One was quite a bit taller than the other, and her hair was caught up in a long ponytail. The other had hers cut at an angle around her chin. He guessed them both to be in their mid-forties, but he had no idea which was the elder.

They both smiled widely at him as they stepped back to let him in.

"It's so nice to meet you in person, Sheriff," the taller one said as she closed the door.

"Ah. Well, thank you, but I'm not the sheriff anymore," he replied. "You can just call me Wyatt."

"We signed the petition about that," said the shorter sister.

"Which petition is that?"

"To get you back into office," the taller sister answered. "That just wasn't right."

"Well, I did resign of my own accord."

"Let's go out on the screened porch," the shorter one suggested. She led the way, with Wyatt in the rear. "We think that's a stupid policy. You two worked together for years without any problems. What if your son wants to be a deputy? He can't?"

They stepped down into a screened porch that was added onto the back of the house. There were plants everywhere, along with several mismatched chairs. An old pine table at one end sat six. There was a green plastic pitcher of tea on the table and three glasses, two of them half-full.

Wyatt waited until the ladies had sat down, one on either end, then he took a seat between them. The taller sister poured him a glass of sweet tea that he didn't like and wouldn't drink. It was a bone of contention between him and Maggie, who thought that any self-respecting person from Virginia ought to be on a steady diet of sweet tea.

Wyatt smiled his thanks for the tea and pulled out a small notebook and pen. "Okay, which one of you is Desiree and which is Dawn?"

"I'm Desiree, she's Dawn," said the taller one.

"DeMott," Wyatt said.

"DeMott deMott," she answered.

"What?"

"I married a deMott," she said simply. "But I'm a big 'D,' big 'M.' He was a big 'M' but a little 'D.'"

"He was," the shorter sister added. *Dawn.*

Wyatt looked at her and then back at Desiree. "So, DeMott-deMott."

"Yes," she said, with an approving smile.

He jotted that down, then looked back at Dawn. "And you're just regular DeMott."

"DeWitt. I married a DeWitt." She smiled politely. "DeMott-DeWitt."

If the circumstances had been different, Wyatt would have known instantly that Maggie and probably a host of other cops had set him up. But circumstances weren't different.

"Okay," he said, jotting that down. "And you were both here at home yesterday when the shooting occurred."

"Oh, we don't live here," Dawn said. "We live in Sopchoppy. We're just house-sitting for our Aunt Louise."

"She's getting a boob job," Desiree explained.

Wyatt nodded. "Can I get your correct addresses, then? In case we need you in court?"

Desiree gave them the address. Apparently, they'd lived together in the house they'd grown up in since their husbands' almost simultaneous deaths. Wyatt was pretty keen to look those up.

"And you were both here when the shooting happened?"

"Yes, but Dawn didn't see it," Desiree said.

"I was back here, working on our scrapbook," Dawn explained. "I didn't go out there until I heard the shot."

"I saw it," Desiree said. "I was getting the mail."

The house was two doors up from the bus stop and across the street. She would have had a good view from the mailbox.

"Can you tell me what you saw?"

"Well, the bus came, and the older kids got off," she answered. "Those boys that started all the crap got off first. Then some other kids. The other boy, he got off last."

Wyatt made notes as she spoke. "What was the dark-haired boy wearing? The one that shot the deputy?"

"He was wearing khaki pants. But they don't call them khakis anymore."

"Cargo pants?" Wyatt asked.

"Yes! Those. They were tan. Tannish. And a red hoodie. I remember thinking it was odd, because it's so hot this week, but it seems like they all wear them, no matter what the weather is."

"He didn't look like a bangclanger, though," Dawn said.

"A what?"

"Gangbanger, Dawn. Geez."

"Give me a break. There's this whole new vocabulary you have to keep straight now," Dawn said. She looked at Wyatt. "What I mean is, not like those kids that wear the hoodies with their pants all falling down. He just looked sporty."

Wyatt nodded. "Okay, so then what happened?"

Desiree sat up straight. "So, I was watching them because the boys all started raising their voices, and then the blond boy shoved the dark-haired kid. Then the deputy, he came around the corner, and he was walking up to them. I thought he was going to bust it up, and he was talking to the dark-haired boy, but then the kid pulled a gun out from under his jacket. His hoodie."

"Did he point it at the deputy?"

"No. No, he was pointing it at the boys. Mainly the blond boy. To be honest, I never saw him point it at the officer. So, I was really surprised he was the one that got shot."

"And the chunky one, you said," Dawn added.

"Yes, the one with the really red hair," Desiree said. "They were standing pretty close together, him and the blond kid, but he was pointing the gun at both of them, kind of."

Wyatt nodded, and Desiree took a sip of her tea. The ice was half-melted and rattled against the glass.

"Anyway, the deputy, he put his hands up; not like 'stick 'em up' but like he was trying to get everybody to calm down. You know?"

Wyatt nodded. "Yeah."

"It scared the crap out of me. But it started looking like the kid was going to put the gun down, and all of a sudden the blond kid throws a backpack at him and the gun went off." She brushed a bit of hair back from her face and Wyatt saw that her hand was trembling just a bit. "I didn't think anybody got shot at first, but then I saw."

"What did you see?" Wyatt asked quietly.

"The deputy, he grabbed his stomach, and then at one point, after the other boys had run away, he was turned so I could see him. He was yelling at the bus driver. I could see blood all over the front of him. It was bad."

Wyatt had seen it, too. She was right. He looked at Dawn. "Were you outside by then?"

"I ran out front after the shot, yes," she said. "Right before the boys ran away. And do you know, it looked to me like the heavy boy was filming it on his phone. I kid you not."

Wyatt felt a powerful heat swirl upward from his stomach to his chest; a current of rage that he had no time to indulge.

"What happened then?"

"Well, I told Dawn to go back into the house because she has such a gentle disposition, and I took out my phone and called 911."

Wyatt waited for her to go on. She put a couple of shaky fingers to her lower lip.

"Then the bus pulled away, and he was...he was running after it, I think. I guess he had a child on the bus because he was calling—" She stopped speaking for a moment, her throat contracting.

"Calling? Calling the bus back?' Wyatt asked.

She shook her head quickly. "No. No, he was yelling 'Daddy's okay'. Over and over."

Her face crumpled, and tears ran down her face. The one with the gentle disposition looked on sympathetically.

"I went back out then," Dawn said. "I was scared for Desi. I saw the deputy on the ground, and people were running out from their houses. I waited with Desi while she talked to 911, and then we ran across the street. We wanted to try to help some way, but we didn't know what to do."

"Everybody was scared," Desiree added, pulling herself up straight. "We didn't know whether to turn him over or bring him inside somewhere. We felt helpless."

"Then the lady officer came running around the corner," Dawn said.

"Yes," her sister said. "She turned him onto his back, and there was so much blood."

"So much."

"And she just whipped off her shirt and tried to stop the bleeding," Desiree said.

"Desi had a shirt on over her tank top, so she took it off and gave it to her."

Wyatt looked from Dawn to Desiree. "You're the one that gave her the shirt."

"Yes?"

Wyatt nodded. "Thank you. She's sorry, but she doesn't know what happened to it."

Desiree waved him away. "Poor thing, I wanted her to put it on, but she misunderstood."

"Wait," Dawn said. "Was that your wife?"

"Yes, ma'am. She appreciated the kindness."

Desiree nodded, and they were quiet for a moment.

"He just kept telling her Daddy was okay," Desiree said after a moment, staring out at the yard. "I'll never get done hearing him say that."

NINE

aggie and Wyatt met at the Petro gas station on 98, just a couple of blocks from Ryan's neighborhood. The station was in a V made by Hwy 98 splitting at Patton Drive. Patton wasn't much of anything except a parallel road right on the bay, allowing access to a couple of boat launches and some rarely-used docks.

Maggie was at the gas pump and she leaned against the side of the Jeep as she filled up and waited for Wyatt to come out with their cold drinks. It was ruthlessly humid, and the very slight breeze off the bay provided her a modicum of relief as she lifted her ponytail to air the back of her neck. A high, dark gray cloud shaped like an anvil hung in the sky out beyond St. George Island. The tip of the anvil pointed roughly west-north-west, promising a pretty good rain across the bridge in Apalach. Maggie wanted to stand out in it.

Wyatt came out of the gas station and headed for the pumps, his remarkably long legs crossing the small parking area in just a few strides. He handed her a giant cup of sweet tea, extra ice. He held a one-liter bottle of Mountain Dew in one hand, and a Snickers bar in the other. He'd already taken a bite.

"You didn't get me a Snickers?"

"Why would I do that?" he asked, leaning against the Jeep.

"Because I'm your wife and you're a gentleman?"

"So I should waste $1.39 buying you a candy bar that you won't eat." He took another bite that reduced the Snickers by half.

"It's a gesture," Maggie said, giving him a small smile. She knew he knew she was baiting him for some banter they both needed.

"So's flipping you off, but that doesn't mean I should do it," Wyatt said. He crumpled the wrapper, tossed it into the waste can, and pulled the suddenly-silent pump out of her tank.

"You and your vegetables and your obsession with oysters and whatnot," he said as he closed her gas tank. "You don't deserve a candy bar. Though you could stand to gain a pound."

"Are you saying I'm too skinny?"

"You're sexy as hell," he answered, kissing the top of her head. "But my left leg weighs more than you do."

"I know. We need a bigger bed."

"Ow."

Maggie took a drink of her tea, then held the cold, sweating cup against her forehead. The mood she was attempting, the few minutes of normalcy she was after, dissipated like dew. She looked out at the bay, then looked up at Wyatt, who was frowning at her.

"We were supposed to be barbecuing with Axel right about now," she said.

"Yeah."

"Dwight is supposed to be in Fort Walton Beach with Amy. It was a surprise."

Wyatt put his soda on the roof of the Jeep, wrapped an arm around her shoulders and pulled her against him. "They'll go when he heals up."

"Yeah."

"Did you get hold of Amy?"

"Yeah," Maggie said. She'd returned Amy's missed call while Wyatt was inside. "Dwight woke up for a minute, but then he got scared because of the restraints they have on him to keep him really still. They put him out." She blew out a breath. "Amy said he didn't realize she was there anyway."

"Because of the drugs?"

Maggie shrugged and shook her head.

"Listen. He's a scrawny little cracker, but he's gonna tough this out," Wyatt said.

Maggie nodded. "I know."

She didn't know, but saying it made it feel like maybe she did.

⚓   ⚓   ⚓

Ryan's chemistry teacher, Jason Carpenter, lived less than fifteen minutes away, on Timber Ridge Court. Maggie and Wyatt drove both vehicles out of habit, in case one of them got a call, and parked in the driveway behind a fairly new Toyota pickup. Timber Ridge was mainly new construction, or at least new within the last decade or so. The homes were modest, and kind of cookie-cutter, but they were nice, and had large lots.

When Maggie got out of the Jeep, she could see two little girls playing in a kiddie pool in the side yard. A slightly-built man in his thirties, with sandy hair and wire-framed glasses, stood near the pool, his eyes going from the driveway to the pool and back again.

Maggie waited a second for Wyatt, then they both walked through well-tended grass to the side of the house.

"Mr. Carpenter?" Wyatt asked.

"Yes. You're Sheriff Hamilton," the man said. His voice was gentle and pleasant.

"Formerly," Wyatt said. The man gave half a nod, like that was up for interpretation.

"This is Lt. Maggie Redmond. Hamilton." Wyatt still got tripped up with that.

Maggie held out her hand. "Mr. Carpenter."

"It's nice to meet you," he said as they shook. "Please call me Jason." He looked over his shoulder at the two little girls, both blond, as the smaller one let out a shriek. "Kylie, give her back the ball."

The older of the two girls, maybe four, stuck out her lower lip, but handed a red ball back to her little sister, then sat down.

"Pretty girls," Maggie said politely.

"Thank you. They're amazing, but they wear me out," Jason answered. "Work's almost a break for me."

"Is your wife or someone here, that could keep an eye on them while we talk?" Wyatt asked.

"No, I'm sorry, there's just the three of us," the man answered. "I can bring them inside if you want to come in the house."

"No, it's okay," Wyatt answered. "We shouldn't need too much of your time."

"Have you found Ryan yet?"

"No, we haven't." Wyatt pulled out his notepad and pen. "Do you have any thoughts about where he might be?"

Jason shook his head. "I'm sorry, I don't. Ryan and I have talked quite a bit outside of the classroom, at school of course, but I don't really know what he does or where his haunts might be outside of school."

"What about friends, classmates? Anyone he hung out with quite a bit?" Wyatt asked.

"Daddy, you water me!" the smaller girl yelled behind him, her smile wide and hopeful.

Jason jerked his head for them to follow him, then picked up a hose with a spray nozzle, and aimed it at the water between her and her sister. The spray bounced up and hit their chests and shoulders, and they squealed appropriately. Maggie wanted to climb in with them, for relief from the heat, and a little kid therapy.

Jason kept squirting the girls as he answered Wyatt. "I know he had a few friends he ate lunch with, a couple of kids he talked to in class, but I don't know who he hung out with."

"He didn't talk to you about any of his friends, what he did over the weekend, that kind of thing?" Maggie asked.

"No, not really." His cargo shorts were getting soaked, but he didn't seem to mind. "He talked to me more about his family than he did his friends."

"What would he tell you?" Wyatt asked.

"Oh, stuff like going out fishing with his uncles and cousins. Going to the beach with his mom. He really likes being a few minutes from the beach. He recently moved here from Orlando." He shrugged. "I guess you know that, though."

"He seem stressed, happy, angry, sad? What's his demeanor like?" Wyatt asked.

"He's pretty laid back, except about his grades," Jason answered. "Outside of the bullying issue."

"He talk to you about that?"

"Quite a bit, yeah, but I was the one that first approached him about it." He switched the hose to his other hand and flexed the one he'd been using. "I could see what was going on."

"What did you see?" Maggie asked, pushing her sunglasses back up her nose. It was slick with sweat, and they slid back down almost immediately.

"Not a lot, but enough to know they were giving him a hard time," he answered. "I'd hear smart remarks or see them at the other end of the hallway, kind of crowding him. I'd see the way Ryan went out of his way to avoid them or become invisible when they were around."

"His mother's been to the principal's office three times, trying to deal with the bullying," Wyatt said.

The man nodded. "Yeah."

"What's bully?" the older girl piped up, squinting up into the sun.

"Nothing, sugar," he answered distractedly. "Let the grown-ups talk, okay?"

"Can I get a snack?"

"In just a few minutes." He stopped spraying. "Why don't you put your Barbies back in the pool, let them swim a little?"

The two girls leaned over the side of the pool and picked up fistfuls of naked Barbie dolls and dumped them into the pool.

"They want water, Daddy," the little one said, and her father started spraying again.

"I know Mrs. Warner tried to get something done about the bullying," he continued. "Although Ryan really didn't want her to. It always got back to the other kids, and it embarrassed him. But it was really getting to him. He couldn't wait to graduate." At this, the teacher's face turned grim, as though realizing that graduation day really wasn't going to mean anything to Ryan Warner anymore.

"I know other officers are speaking with the principal today, but can you kind of give us a synopsis of her take on things?"

"She's trying really hard to create a good environment for these kids," Jason said. "She works really hard at it. We've all had lots of classes and workshops on bullying and sexual harassment and all of that kind of thing," the teacher answered. "But between the school board and the State of Florida and the Department of Education and every other CYA organism, we're kind of crippled when it comes to these things."

"How so?" Wyatt asked him.

"Everything's so politically correct, everybody's all worried about rights and lawsuits and countersuits and media and all this other stuff, and everybody's so scared of taking action that we're failing the kids."

He'd gotten pretty animated during that little bit. Maggie found herself liking him. She hoped he'd still be at the school when Kyle started high school. Clearly, he felt very strongly about kids.

"So what does that translate to?" Wyatt asked, then held up a hand. "That's not exactly how I meant to phrase that. What I mean is, how doe the politics impact what the principal is doing about bullying?"

Jason shrugged. "Gotta have witnesses, preferably adult witnesses. Staff. Even then, it doesn't always mean expulsion. Sometimes, depending on the circumstances, it's a suspension first. And even then, if there's a physical altercation, usually both parties end up suspended. The kids aren't allowed to defend themselves, either." He sighed and dragged a hand over his head. "That's what zero tolerance actually translates to."

Wyatt nodded. He knew a lot of this, some in abstract terms, some more concrete. His office had been called out to the school to break up fights many times, and most of those times, all they could do was break it up and tell the kids to straighten up. As of last school year, the Sheriff's Office had two deputies assigned solely to the high school five days a week. They didn't have metal detectors yet, but they'd been approved and budgeted and were supposed to be in by the fall.

"Mr. Carpenter, why do you think Ryan took that gun to school Thursday?" Maggie asked him.

He looked at her for a long moment before answering. "I don't know. When I heard that he had, it just blew me away." He stopped, swallowed hard. "Of course, the shooting. I don't really know how or why that happened, except that I can tell you that Ryan just isn't the kind of kid who hates cops or has some kind of vendetta."

"But he did take the gun," Wyatt said quietly.

"He did, yeah. And I don't know why," Jason said. "Look, as a teacher—as a *parent* for crying out loud—I can't excuse what he did. Kids cannot have guns. Kids cannot bring guns to school or try to solve problems with weapons. They *can't*. I really like Ryan. I'm sure this isn't what you want to hear, because your fellow officer was shot, probably a friend, but Ryan really has always been a good kid."

Wyatt nodded, then looked over at Maggie. "You have any other questions?"

Maggie shook her head. "No." She looked at Jason Carpenter. "Thank you for your time." She started to turn away, then looked back at him. "Thank you for teaching."

He seemed surprised by that. He nodded, shook Wyatt's hand, then watched them as they walked to the driveway.

Maggie and Wyatt stopped at Maggie's Jeep. She opened the door to let out some of the death-dealing heat for a minute.

"What do you think?" Wyatt asked as her phone buzzed.

She pulled it out of her pocket. It was Myles. "Hey, Myles, what's up?"

"Mags, we have a problem," he said. "The Nichols parents don't know where Adrian Nichols is."

"What do you mean? Hold on." She looked over at Jason and his girls, then up at Wyatt. "Let's get in the car so I can put him on speaker."

"What's up?" Wyatt asked as he walked around to the other side.

"I'm not sure." They both got in the car, leaving the doors open. Maggie turned on the engine and started the air. "Myles, I'm putting you on speaker so Wyatt can hear." She tapped the icon. "Go ahead."

"Yeah, so Nichols is missing," Myles repeated.

"Since when?" Maggie asked him.

"Not sure. The mother went to bed with a stress headache last night about seven. She said the kid told her he was going out. The dad had the shrimp boat out all night and went to bed as soon as he got home this morning. He didn't wake up till I got here."

"Was he on foot, with friends or what?" Wyatt asked.

"He left by himself, in his car."

"If he has a car, why does he ride a bus to school?" Maggie asked.

"Well, he keeps getting grounded from the car, plus he won't hold a job and the dad's stingy with gas money," Miles answered.

"So what are we thinking?' Wyatt asked.

"I don't know what we're thinking," Myles answered, frustration coming through loud and clear. "I mean, we're not even charging him with anything. Yet. So why split?"

"Maybe he just crashed at a friend's house?" Maggie offered.

"So far, none of the friends the mom's gotten in touch with."

"Where's the Newman kid?" Wyatt asked.

"Oh, Quincy just sent his happy ass home," Myles said. "He and his parents got pulled down to the SO, and Bledsoe gave him the works. Don't know if he had any legal standing, but he made him take the YouTube channel down. That video's all over the place, though, you know that."

Maggie felt sick to her stomach about that. Amy had told her and Wyatt this morning that she'd heard about it, but her father convinced her not to watch it. Maggie doubted that would last long, though. Maggie had unintentionally witnessed her husband's violent death, but if she hadn't, and it had been out on some video, she knew she would have been irresistibly drawn to see for herself.

"Okay, well," Wyatt said. "If anybody knows where this kid is holed up, it's Newman. We're gonna take a run over there. Text me the address."

"You got it," Myles said, and disconnected.

Wyatt looked at Maggie. "You've been a parent for eighteen years," he said. "I don't know how you're not a pill head."

CHAPTER

TEN

aggie followed Wyatt to the Newman residence. She was surprised to find that the Newmans lived in one of the very few wealthy neighborhoods in Eastpoint, right near East Bay, which separated Eastpoint and Apalach.

The house was large, without being grotesque. There was nothing ostentatious about the brick rancher with the white columns, but the professional landscaping, three car garage, and the location made the financial status of the Newman family very clear.

She and Wyatt got out and headed for the house. There was a brick-paved porch that ran the width of the house, with four white rockers that didn't look like they saw much use. A few large pots of flowers were strategically placed on the porch and near the steps, but the porch felt like it was strictly for show.

Wyatt rang the doorbell. They could hear the tinny chiming inside. After a moment, the door was opened by a man in his late fifties, with a rapidly receding hairline and no discernible chin.

"Yes?"

"Mr. Newman?" Wyatt asked.

The man looked at Wyatt, then Maggie. "Yes," he answered to Maggie, though Wyatt had asked the question.

"I'm Wyatt Hamilton with the Sheriff's Office," Wyatt said politely. "This is Lt. Redmond."

Maggie noticed he intentionally used her maiden name.

"Yes," the man said, his face instantly solemn, and a little nervous. "May I help you?"

"Is your son at home?"

"Well, yes, but we've just come from the Sheriff's Office," Newman said. "Stuart took that YouTube channel down."

"Yes, I understand, but we need to speak with him for a few minutes," Wyatt said, nicely but firmly.

The man hesitated a moment, then held the door open and stepped back. "Okay."

Wyatt and Maggie entered a hallway with a floor of gray stone, bright white walls, and carefully arranged oddments of furniture. There were a few family pictures on the walls of the long hallway, all of them professionally done, but the majority of the wall art was actual art.

There were several white double doors on either side of the hall, which ended in an open-concept sort of great room. The back of the room looked like it was made up entirely of windows overlooking the bay.

"My wife and son are on the back patio," Newman said. He tucked his hands into the pockets of his green golf pants, then took them out again. Maggie wondered why he'd been golfing when his son was in the middle of a serious situation.

"You have a very nice home," Wyatt said politely. Maggie knew he hated it.

"Thank you."

"What do you do?"

"I'm a tax attorney," the man answered.

"That makes sense."

They followed the man down the hall and into the large great room. As it turned out, there was a big fireplace in the center of the back wall, with the windows filling in the rest. As they followed the man toward the sliding glass doors, Maggie saw a woman and young man sitting at a white wrought iron table on the expansive back patio. There was a pool beyond it, and beyond that a narrow lawn that led the eye to the bay.

The woman was facing the house, and she looked up as they approached the glass. She had dark red hair, in an expensive-looking bob, and eyebrows that had to consist exclusively of pencil. She was attractive anyway, in a matronly, country club kind of way.

Stuart Newman appeared to be eating a late lunch or an early dinner, and he looked up from his plate as the sliding door opened. Maggie and Wyatt followed the man out.

"The police have some more questions," Mr. Newman said, his tone a mixture of weariness and anxiety.

"Now what?" Stuart asked, clearly exasperated.

Maggie disliked him instantaneously. He was not an attractive kid; quite a bit overweight and with bright red hair that was wild to the point of ugly. His looks wouldn't have meant much if he didn't have such an angry, entitled look on his face, and a clear ring of arrogance to his tone.

"Hi, Stuart," Wyatt said almost cheerfully, and Maggie knew the kid was done.

"Who are you?"

"Stuart," the father said quietly. The kid didn't seem to hear him.

"I'm Wyatt Hamilton with the Sheriff's Office, and this is Lt. Redmond," Wyatt answered. "We'd like to ask you some questions about Adrian Nichols."

"Well, why don't you ask him, 'cause I've been at your office for the last three hours or something and now I'm trying to eat."

"Stuart," the father said again, to the same effect. The mother hadn't said a word yet.

"Nobody seems to be able to find your friend Adrian," Wyatt said. "You know where he is?"

The kid didn't really try to hide his amusement. "You mean, like, the whole Sheriff's department can't find him?"

"I mean his parents don't know where he is," Wyatt said. "No one's seen him since yesterday evening."

The kid looked under his bread and then at his mother. "Why did you put brown mustard on this? You know it gives me heartburn."

"We were out of the yellow," she answered. Her voice was quiet, and while not quite timid, it wasn't exactly confident, either.

"Geez."

"Stuart? You know where Adrian is?" Wyatt asked.

"No, man," Stuart said. "I don't."

"You sure? You're his best friend, right?"

"Yeah, but I'm not his girlfriend." He finally looked up from his plate. "I don't know where he is."

"Where does he hang out when he's not at home?"

The kid shrugged his large shoulders. "Wherever."

"Stuart, please show these officers some respect," the father said quietly. "A deputy has been shot."

"Well, I didn't shoot him, so…" The kid pushed back his chair and heaved himself out of it. "I haven't talked to Adrian since yesterday, and I took down my YouTube channel. So leave me alone already."

Maggie couldn't believe the nerve on the kid. She'd seen it in many adults, but never in a high school kid. Not with the law, and not with a lawman the size of Wyatt.

The kid headed toward them, as though to go into the house. Wyatt held up a finger when the kid was almost abreast of him.

"How old are you, Stuart?"

The kid's chest got a little higher. "Eighteen."

Wyatt smiled and put a hand on his shoulder. "Excellent! Come with me for a minute."

He started leading the kid out to the yard.

"Uh, shouldn't we be present?" the father asked.

"He's eighteen," Wyatt said. "We'll just be a minute."

The father looked at Maggie as she started after them. "He's not going to hurt him or anything, is he?"

"No. No, not at all," Maggie answered. "Sometimes it's just better to speak privately."

She knew for a fact that Wyatt wanted to toss this kid around for a while, and she'd seen him do more than a little damage more than a few times. But she'd never known someone so even-tempered, so able to choose when to let his anger, and his might, have their own way.

She hurried to catch up with them. Stuart was mumbling, but she didn't catch what he was saying. She had almost caught up when Wyatt stopped and faced the kid and popped his fists on his hips.

"Listen up, kid. You not only bully and harass people, but you make and upload videos you have no business making or uploading—"

"Hey, I know my First Amendment rights, so don't even," the kid said. "And my channel happens to be popular."

"You don't know the first thing about the First Amendment," Wyatt said evenly.

"My father's a lawyer."

"He's a CPA with a law degree," Wyatt snapped. "So let me give you some legal advice that's actually applicable to your situation. You might not get charged for putting up that video of Ryan Warner. You might not even get charged for uploading to the public the shooting of a Franklin County Sheriff's Deputy. A deputy whose *family* didn't need to see their father or husband or son get a bullet in the abdomen because he was trying to help some kids."

"Hey, it's news," the kid said. "That's what my channel is about, stuff that's interesting or news, and people watch my stuff!"

Wyatt leaned in. "You think you're a celebrity because you have a channel any third-grader or barely functioning alcoholic could create? You think getting a bunch of clicks means people are actually interested in *you*? You're a snowflake in a hailstorm, kid, and your videos are not news or entertainment, or anything else that means anything."

"I don't have to listen to you lecture me, man." Stuart's face had turned red, the red of humiliation and frustration.

"I'm almost done talking," Wyatt said. "You upload one more video, and I will make damn sure you wait inside Franklin Correctional while we let the DA and your lawyer argue about whether the charges will stick."

"You can't do that," the kid said.

"Don't put too much money on that," Wyatt said. "Although, by the time Dwight Shultz's attorney gets done suing you and your parents for emotional duress, you probably won't have much."

With that, Wyatt spun around and headed for the patio, where Mr. and Mrs. Newman were waiting.

Wyatt handed Mr. Newman his card. "Please call me if you hear anything about where Adrian Nichols might be," he said.

"Yes, I will."

"Clearly Stuart can afford a car," Wyatt said. "Why was he on that school bus?"

"He failed his exam again," the man answered. "His mother has offered to pick him up, but he prefers to ride the bus and spend time at Adrian's house."

Wyatt sighed. "Thank you for your time."

Mr. Newman walked them out and shut the door quietly behind them. Maggie didn't speak until they were in the driveway.

"The next time I feel like I'm too hard on the kids, remind me what indulgence looks like," she said.

"Okay. Do you think they specifically asked the adoption agency for a redneck baby?"

ELEVEN

The storm foretold by the small army of anvils had been overhead for an hour. At only 7pm, it shouldn't have been dark yet, but it nearly was.

Maggie was late getting home and starting dinner. She and Wyatt met with most of the rest of the team to compare notes and next steps, then they'd drove together to Port St. Joe. This time, they'd been allowed to step into Dwight's room for just a minute, even though he was in the ICU.

He'd been deeply tanned since Maggie had known him, when she'd been a teenager helping her Daddy out on the oyster beds, and he'd been just a little kid, helping his father sort shrimp by size. Sometimes, both of their fathers would be at Boudreaux's receiving docks at the same time, and Maggie would walk little Dwight over to the soda machine at Scipio Creek Marina, so they

could get some cold Dr. Peppers while the men trans-
acted business.

The first thing Maggie noticed when she stepped
quietly into Dwight's hospital room was that he was
frighteningly pale. As she and Wyatt stopped at his
bedside, she also noticed that Dwight's Adam's apple
was unnaturally still. Dwight was always either chat-
tering or swallowing nervously, that little knot of car-
tilage constantly bobbing, like a buoy in rough waters.

They had stayed for just a few minutes, offering Amy
and Dwight's parents what superficial comfort they
could, then driven the half hour back to Apalach in
silence.

Maggie stared out the window over the sink as she
rinsed the butter lettuce that she'd cut from the garden.
She hadn't minded getting wet to do it, after drowning
in the heat all day.

She had the windows and sliding glass doors open, in
spite of the heat and humidity, so that she could listen
to her storm. They were all her storms; her favorite
weather since she was a baby. The lightning, the thunder,
the sheets of rain. Even after fighting for her life during
a hurricane the year before, she considered the storms
her special friends.

The rain was starting to die down, the air beginning
to cool a bit now that the day had gotten something out
of its system. Stoopid stood at the sliding glass door, beak

to screen, testing the barometric pressure and warbling in the general direction of the chicken run, where the girls were huddled single file beneath the overhangs.

Maggie didn't hear Kyle come in from the living room, and was surprised when he leaned against the counter next to the sink.

"Hey, Mom."

"Hey, bud," she said. "How's it going?"

She never got over Kyle. His almost-black hair and sensuously-long eyelashes were directly from his father, the boy she'd loved since they'd been twelve years old. A little younger than Kyle was now, she realized with a start. Kyle was a constant reminder of someone who had been her very best friend her whole life, more friend than lover, she'd eventually realized, but he was also incredible in his own right. He was funny and smart and very often seemed like he had the simple wisdom of an old man.

"Okay, I guess," he said quietly. "I'm done with my homework."

"What's the matter?" she asked him. She carried the colander of lettuce over to the island, and he turned around to face her.

"I watched the video," he said after a moment. "Do you think that was disrespectful?"

Maggie swallowed hard. "Of Dwight?"

"Yeah." He used his thumbnail to scrape at a ding in the heavily-varnished barnwood counter.

"Well, I guess that would depend on why you watched it," Maggie answered. She had picked up her chef's knife, but it hovered in place over her cutting board.

Kyle shrugged one shoulder, that way a kid does when he knows what an answer is but doesn't know how it'll be received.

"I don't know," Kyle said finally. "I just couldn't help wanting to see what really happened. It was going around and around in my head, anyway, wondering. Picturing it."

"How did it make you feel to watch it?"

"I cried."

"Good," she said softly.

"It's not that I was watching it just out of curiosity, or because it would be freaky to see somebody get shot," Kyle said insistently. "I just felt like…" He shrugged again, looking uncomfortable.

"Like what?" Maggie turned to the cutting board and started slicing tomatoes, trying to give him the illusion of privacy that he needed to be frank.

"I know it's kinda weird, but I felt like Dwight had been all alone. You know, like he was all alone when it happened," Kyle said.

Maggie's hand decelerated, and she was slicing in slow motion.

"I felt like, if I watched it, it would be like someone who cared about him was with him," her son said.

Maggie breathed in deeply through her nose, and slowly used her knife to slide the tomatoes aside.

"I know it's not logical," Kyle said, "but that's just what I felt like."

Maggie looked over at him. A wisp of a breeze came through the kitchen window behind him, drifted through the silky hair at the top of his head.

"It doesn't have to be logical to be right," Maggie said quietly.

Kyle chewed at the corner of his lower lip, the way she did when she was thinking, but didn't know she did.

"So, you don't think it was disrespectful?"

"No. I don't know if it was wise; I wish you hadn't seen it," she answered. "But it wasn't disrespectful."

He nodded slightly. "Okay."

He looked down at the hardwood floor, rubbed it with his bare toe. Maggie put down the knife and started tearing the lettuce into a bowl.

"How long till dinner?" he asked her.

"Just a few minutes. I'm just waiting for the corn chowder to thicken up a bit."

"Okay. Do you want some help?"

"No, thanks," she answered distractedly. "Actually, could you take the trash bins out to the road? I'm gonna run some scraps out to the girls and put them inside."

It was a bit of a trek to the road from the house, and her parents had a beaten-up old golf cart they'd been given which they had used to haul the trash and recycling bins. Maggie and Wyatt just kept the bins on the back of the cart so nobody had to lift the full bins.

"Yeah, okay," Kyle said.

Maggie finished tearing the lettuce, dumped it into the salad bowl, then grabbed a small Tupperware from the counter that held grapefruit skins and some soft blueberries from breakfast, wilted lettuce leaves, and the corn cobs left from making the chowder.

She grabbed her phone from the island and slid it into her back pocket, then went out the sliding door to the back deck. She didn't bother trying to bring Stoopid out; he was too good for the rain anymore.

By the time she got to the run, the girls had clustered in front of the chicken wire door, guessing noisily at what she might have in the bowl this evening.

"Hey, ladies," she said gently. "Back up."

The door opened inward. Most of the hens backed up. The ones who were senile or just a little slow had to be moved back by the door, like protesters behind a police barricade.

Maggie stepped in and, tapping at the bowl with her fingernail, preceded everybody to the ramp that led up into the coop. As several hens either ran up or flew in, she tossed the snacks inside. Once everyone was in and focused on the produce, looking like old ladies bobbing for apples, Maggie lifted the ramp to close the coop and pushed the wooden toggle over.

She walked over to the waterer and made sure there was plenty of water and a minimum of poop, then she leaned up against the side of the coop and pulled out her phone.

It seemed there were plenty of videos of cops getting shot or shot at. It took Maggie just a few minutes, using three different search phrases, to find Dwight. The thumbnail was of a frightened-looking Ryan Warner pointing a gun somewhere between the camera and the ground. The title of the video was "Raw Footage!!! COP SHOT IN FRONT OF MY EYES!!!!"

A flash of pure rage surged from Maggie's feet to her forehead. Her heart pounded with it, and she closed her eyes as she pictured herself kicking Stuart Newman all over his manicured lawn. She didn't remember ever wanting to beat someone so young, but she knew she did now.

For a minute, Maggie tried to talk herself into going into the house. Then she tapped at the screen and watched Ryan's head turn to his right. The camera did, too, and there was Dwight, hands in the air, his uniform spotless and hanging just a bit from his wiry frame.

The sound wasn't great, even though Maggie did have it turned down a bit, out of fear. But she could hear.

"Son, what's your name?" Dwight was asking Ryan.

"Ryan." His voice wasn't what Maggie had expected. He looked and sounded younger somehow.

"Come on, Ryan," Dwight said kindly. "It'll be okay."

The camera zoomed out jerkily, and now Maggie could see both Ryan and Dwight in the same frame, and the back end of the school bus.

"Ryan, we're sorry, man," said someone close to the camera.

Dwight glanced toward the camera. Maggie tapped at the screen in a near panic. She wanted Dwight to stay that way, to never get to the point where he wasn't okay anymore. But then she took a shaky breath and tapped it again.

Suddenly a big gray blur flew into the shot, everything went shaky, and Maggie heard the .22.

In her mind's eye, she could see herself three blocks away, paying their bill and telling Lynn that Dwight was getting promoted in less than an hour. Looking up quickly as the shot reached her ears.

In the video, kids were screaming. Little kids. The camera stopped jerking around, though it wobbled a little. Dwight was standing there with a look of amazement on his face, blood already seeping out between his fingers as he held his hand to his stomach. Maggie put a hand over her mouth as Dwight looked over at the camera. Ryan ran off to the right, the gun still in his hand.

Dwight looked toward the bus, then raised his free arm and yelled. "Sam, go on! Go on around the corner!"

The bus started moving, and Maggie could still hear the kids screaming as Dwight took a few steps, like he was about to run.

"It's okay, baby," he called. "Daddy's okay."

Maggie felt a wave of nausea, felt her throat thickening as Dwight staggered a bit.

"Daddy's okay," he was yelling, and then he fell face first toward the ground, but the camera suddenly jerked away and then went dark. Maggie never saw Dwight hit the ground.

She jerked open the door to the chicken run and just made it out before she threw up her sweet tea.

Maggie stuck her head under the spray of beautifully hot water and started running her hands through her hair to rinse out the conditioner. "What?" she asked.

Wyatt took his toothbrush out of his mouth. "I said, Amy just texted. They're going ahead with the surgery. 7am."

"Okay," Maggie answered. She opened the curtain enough to look out at him. "Remind me to send her a text when I get out."

Wyatt looked away from the phone on the vanity and went back to brushing his teeth. Then he turned the faucet on.

"Wyatt!"

He winced and turned the faucet back off with a jerk. "Sorry, I forgot."

He spat into the sink, then wiped his hands on the legs of the black drawstring shorts he was wearing for pajamas. His favorite old Bama shirt was a faded red, the Crimson Tide logo barely visible.

Maggie shut off the water, and Wyatt grabbed a towel from the rack and held it open for her as she flung open the shower curtain. She turned around in it, then knotted it over her chest.

"Are you single?" Wyatt asked her.

"No."

"Rats."

Maggie's phone buzzed from the floor where her jeans and t-shirt where piled. She bent and slipped it out of her back pocket. It was an SO landline. "Maggie."

"Maggie, it's Quincy," she heard. "There's another YouTube video. It looks like Adrian Nichols is with Ryan Warner."

"What??"

"What?" Wyatt echoed.

Maggie tapped the speaker icon, and Quincy's voice became tinny and bounced off the bathroom walls.

"Uh, it looks like we might have a hostage situation."

"Which one's the hostage?" Wyatt asked.

"Nichols, believe it or not," Quincy answered.

"Is Newman there?" Wyatt asked.

"Wait a minute," Maggie said, handing Wyatt her phone. "I thought that YouTube channel was shut down."

"Yeah, this isn't Newman's channel. It's Adrian's."

Maggie dropped her towel and started pulling on her blue-striped pajama pants. "What's the name of it?"

"I'll text you the URL in just a second," Quincy says. "We're gonna pull it up on the conference room monitor, see if we can see where it was filmed. Meanwhile, we're thinking he used his cell to upload it, so we're trying to get a ping on it again."

"Okay, call us back if you do," Wyatt said, disconnecting and opening the bathroom door as soon as Maggie had pulled her ancient Papa Joe's tank top over her head.

She followed him as he stalked down the hall, past Sky's closed door, and went to Kyle's half-open one. He rapped on the door once out of habit, as he was already walking in. Kyle was on his laptop at his desk.

"Kyle, buddy, we need to use your laptop," Wyatt said quickly.

"What's up?"

"We need to see something," Maggie said.

"Did I do something?" Kyle asked, getting up.

"No, buddy, we just need to borrow it," Wyatt said.

He and Maggie were both Luddites, neither one of them fond of computers except for work. Maggie's hard drive had been corrupted several weeks back, and she wasn't too motivated to fix it. Wyatt hadn't seen his power cord since they'd moved.

"What are you looking at?" Kyle asked as Wyatt sat down in his chair.

"A YouTube video, but I don't think you should watch it."

"If you mean Dwight, I already did," Kyle said softly.

Wyatt looked over his shoulder at him. "You shouldn't have," he said gently.

"What's going on?" Sky was leaning in the doorway.

Maggie turned to look at her daughter. "Ryan and Adrian are in a YouTube video together."

"What do you mean?"

"Somebody uploaded a video," Wyatt said, minimizing the Wikipedia page on tropical weather patterns and pulling up YouTube. "Maggie, do you have that URL?"

Maggie had her text screen open. She put her phone down next to the laptop so Wyatt could read it. "Maybe we should just watch it on my phone."

"I want to see it big," he replied. "See if we can see any details, see where they are."

"They're doing that at the SO right now," she said unnecessarily.

"I know." He looked over at her. "Should the kids go into the kitchen or what?"

"No, it's nothing violent," Maggie said. "Quincy would have said so."

"Okay."

He hit ENTER and YouTube came up. The still shot from the video was of Adrian Nichols' angry face. The title of the video was "No More Bullies."

Wyatt took a deep breath, let it out in a *whoosh* and clicked.

"This is *bull*, man!" Adrian Nichols barked, but there was uncertainty in his eyes.

"Do it," Ryan's voice said, close to the camera.

"Look, we were just messing around," Adrian said. "You're the one that blew everything up into some big mess!"

"You haven't been *messing around* for a year, Adrian!" Ryan yelled. "You've been making every single day hell for me."

"You need a thicker skin, man!" Adrian said, a little desperation creeping in, despite the bravado coming out of his mouth. "Guys get razzed all the time."

Maggie got distracted from the screen when she sensed movement beside her. She looked. Sky had come to stand next to her, her eyes glued to the monitor.

"This isn't about getting razzed and you know it," Ryan was saying. "Hitting isn't razzing. Knocking people down isn't razzing. Closing their fingers in lockers isn't razzing."

"That wasn't me, that was Newman," Adrian said.

"You're the instigator! You're the one that started all of it, and you're the one that kept it going!"

"Yeah?" Adrian yelled. There was more fear in his voice than anger. "Well, I'm not the one who shot the cop, though, am I?"

There was no answer for a moment. They could hear a chair or some piece of wood creaking as Adrian appeared to shift position. The camera only covered him from his upper chest to his face. With the camera that close, it was impossible to see if he was restrained in any way, or to make out any details behind him, other than a scarred brick wall.

The camera was jostled a bit, and Maggie could hear movement close by. Ryan.

"I want you to tell everybody what you did."

"You just said it, man!" Adrian was sweating. The sheen on his upper lip was magnified by the light coming from roughly overhead.

"You say it!" Ryan yelled. "Come on, you've had so much to say all year long. All your hard work making me freaking miserable and you don't want to brag about it? You want to be a big deal on YouTube, right? Talk."

"Come on, Ryan," Adrian said, more quietly. "Just—come on, put the gun down and go. Or let me go. Just—everybody hears you, okay?"

There was another moment of silence. Then, "It doesn't matter if everybody hears."

There was shaky movement of the camera again, and then it was Ryan's face on the screen. Too close. He looked so different from the last time she'd seen his face, just a few hours ago, that Maggie was shocked. She couldn't even pinpoint what it was. He looked haggard, exhausted and ten years older, yet ten years younger at the same time. Looking straight into his eyes this way, so close, she felt him as an actual, living, breathing, frightened kid for the first time.

"I didn't mean to hurt that police officer," he said. "Watch the video these guys plastered all over the internet. I didn't mean it. He was trying to help me."

The video stopped, and they were looking at Adrian's angry face again. The room seemed so quiet suddenly.

Wyatt stood up. "I'm gonna go call in, see how they're doing with his phone."

He walked out of the room. Kyle sat back down in his chair and closed the screen. Maggie turned to go and almost bumped into Sky.

"Somebody needs to find him, Mom," she said quietly. "I've probably only said hello to him like five times since that first week of school, but he's never looked like that. Or sounded like that."

"We're trying."

"Can't you use Find My Phone or something?" Maggie had it for Sky and Kyle's iPhones; she had since they'd started going places without her.

"For some reason, that's not an option for us. I don't remember why. There are a couple of guys trying to locate his phone by what cell towers he pings off of, but he's been turning off his phone," Maggie said.

Sky looked at her for a moment. "Okay," she said, and walked out of the room.

The mood around the conference table the next morning was grim. Dwight was in surgery, and everyone kept one eye on their watches or cell phones as they waited for news that wasn't going to come anytime soon.

Instead of an armed kid who'd accidentally shot an officer and a runaway kid hiding from the law, they now had a kid with a hostage. Judging by the video, Ryan still had his gun. Judging by the fact that no one had seen or heard from Adrian Nichols, he still had him, too.

"Okay, so the video," Bledsoe was saying from the head of the table. "It was uploaded to Adrian's YouTube Channel, as most of you know, I guess. So, we can assume that Ryan is able to…what do we want to say? Manipulate the kid. Since the kid mentioned the gun in the video, we can figure that's how."

That seemed pretty obvious, but Maggie was trying to like him because of what he'd done with Dwight's benefits.

"Okay. The kid apparently uploaded using his cell phone, because we have a ping from the tower over off Bluff Road a little before the video was posted. Unfortunately, the phone was turned off by then, and didn't ping anywhere else, but we've got a six people assigned just to Bluff Road to see if we can find the kids out there."

Maggie's old house, where her parents now lived, was at the end of Bluff Road. It ran about five miles out of town, and besides all the houses out there, there were also acres and acres of woods.

"That's a tough place to search with just that to go on," she said, thinking out loud.

"Yeah, well, I didn't get a chance to ask the kid to do it downtown," Bledsoe said irritably. "Let's continue. We have a BOLO out for Adrian Nichols' car, and we also have watches on each and every gas station in the area. Myles says this kid didn't usually have much gas in the tank."

"Do we know if Ryan has any money on him?" Wyatt asked.

"No. His mom said he had a little bit in the bank, and had about $85 dollars saved up in cash, towards a new laptop for school, but she doesn't know where he kept it, so she doesn't know if it's gone."

"What about the money in the bank?" Quincy asked.

"Still there," Bledsoe answered. "Okay. Wyatt. Channel Four wants to do a story, and they've already been in touch with both mothers. Adrian's mother doesn't want to go on TV. Ryan's mother does. She's hoping he'll watch it and turn himself in."

"Okay," Wyatt said cautiously.

"Okay, so you have a press conference out front here at 3:15."

"I think my time would be better spent out there looking for these kids, don't you?"

Bledsoe had shown himself to be a real press hound in the several months that he'd been there. Wyatt would be okay if there was no press at all.

"I think I still need you to do your regular job," Bledsoe said testily. "I've got the governor up my butt about kids who shoot cops and manage to hide from beaucoup law enforcement officers in a town that doesn't even have a Walmart."

"We don't want a Walmart," Wyatt said slowly, and Maggie knew he was put out by about Bledsoe's tone and was trying to tick him off.

"Can we play around next week?" Bledsoe asked.

Wyatt picked up his Mountain Dew and took a long drink.

"3:15," Bledsoe repeated. "Out front. Now, let's all get going and get this crap over and done with before we all get fired. You've got your to-do lists, let's go do."

Wyatt stood, and waited for Maggie to grab her file folder and phone. Once Bledsoe was out of the room, Myles looked at Wyatt. "Boss? What do you give for odds we can get *both* of these kids back in one piece?"

Wyatt sighed as he followed Maggie to the door and held it open for her.

"I don't know, Myles," he said. "But let's try and keep that as our main priority."

As Maggie stepped out into the hall, she heard raised voices at the other end of it. "Sounds like somebody's not too happy to be here this morning," she said.

"I'm not too happy about being here."

They rounded the corner and saw Bledsoe and a couple of deputies standing with their backs to them.

Facing them was an angry looking man in his late thirties or early forties. He had blond hair that had clearly been bleached blonder than birth by the sun. There was at least two days' growth of beard on his deeply tanned face. Maggie pegged him as a commercial fisherman though she didn't know his face.

"Aw, crap," Myles said behind them.

"I want to know why everybody's talking about finding this Warner loser and nobody's telling me what they're doing to find *my* kid!" the man was yelling.

"Nichols kid's father?" Wyatt asked.

"Yeah," Myles answered. "Which is why I have to go do stuff."

Myles turned around and went back the way they'd come. Maggie and Wyatt joined the little group at the end of the hall.

"Mr. Nichols, I told you on the phone last night, and I'm telling you this morning, we are looking for each of these boys with equal urgency," Bledsoe was saying.

"Yeah? That's not how it looks from where I'm standing."

"I'm sorry if you can't see that, sir, and I sympathize with your concern for your boy, but standing here in the hallway isn't helping us find *anybody's* son."

"How come you're going on TV about this Ryan kid, but you're not putting the word out about Adrian? Explain that. I saw the commercial this morning."

"Mr. Nichols, the press asked your wife to participate and she declined," Bledsoe said with a sigh.

Nichols glanced over at Maggie while Bledsoe was talking, and the distaste with which he looked at her let her know two things: he didn't like cops and he especially didn't like women cops. Those guys were pretty easy to spot.

He looked back at Bledsoe. "Well, tell the reporters I'll talk to them."

Bledsoe sighed. "Mr. Nichols, that's something you'll have to talk to them about yourself," he said. "Now, I need you to go on and let us get back to work. Finding *your* son."

The man looked Bledsoe up and down, then turned and headed for the door, his heavy boots making him sound bigger than he was.

Bledsoe turned around and saw Maggie and Wyatt. "Now that another five minutes has been wasted, let's get back to it."

"It was kind of nice of him to stop in, though," Wyatt said quietly to Bledsoe's back. "We should have people over more often."

CHAPTER
THIRTEEN

Apalachicola Chocolate & Coffee was in a restored building on Market Street, amidst several boutiques, cafes, artisanal stores and art galleries. Maggie just called it Apalachicola Coffee, because chocolate was irrelevant. She'd been going there since it had opened.

It was 2:40, and she had five minutes left to live if she didn't get her latte. She and Wyatt walked up the sidewalk, and Wyatt pulled open the door.

"Do me a favor, let him make my coffee before you start giving him a hard time," he said under his breath.

"What?!" Maggie stumbled over the little transition strip she always forgot was there. "I treat the guy like a Maharishi just so I can get a cup of decent coffee."

She and the new owner, Kirk Lynch, had gotten off on the wrong foot about a year ago, and never switched over to the other one. Wyatt accused her of liking the battle of sarcasm she had to go through every day, but Wyatt was a jerk.

There were a few customers milling around the gelato and chocolate counters on the left side of the shop, but Maggie only had eyes for the coffee counter at the back. There were two customers there already, a young couple who were clearly just back from the beach. They both wore SGI tank tops over their bathing suits, and the back of her shorts sported a smiling dolphin.

As Maggie and Wyatt got into line behind them, Kirk looked over their heads at Maggie. His face was artful in its complete lack of expression. He had his graying, light brown hair tied up in a ponytail, and a Grateful Dead bandana on his head.

"What about the vanilla chai latte?" the young woman was asking her companion.

The one thing Maggie couldn't stand, besides everything else, was people who thought spices and flavorings and Grape-Nuts or whatever had any business being anywhere near high-quality coffee. Why Kirk allowed it confounded her, though he whined about the market and trends and other crap Maggie couldn't care less about.

"I don't know, babe," the young man said, with a tinge of whining himself. "I'm thinking about getting one of those truffles over there. I think the flavors would clash, don't you?"

Kirk looked at Maggie, made a show of looking at his watch, and then smiled at his customers. "Would you like to try one of the truffles, just to make sure?"

Maggie's lower jaw dropped just a bit, and she looked up at Wyatt, then busied herself looking at the huge burlap coffee bags that hung on the wall and the sign that said to grab life by the beans.

"Uh, you know, that would be awesome," the young woman said, sounding excited. Maggie was so pleased for her.

Kirk raised his eyebrows at Maggie, like an extra-polite bullfighter swinging a red blanket. "Lemme just get Spaz," he said mildly, his eyes on Maggie, and she felt her chest cave in.

"Spaz!" Kirk called over to the chocolate counter.

Spaz was a man in his sixties or seventies, with dyed blue-black hair and an expression of perpetual disenchantment. He also moved at the speed of wood. He looked up from the counter he was wiping and dropped his mouth open in silent reply.

"Would you bring these folks one of the almond truffles we just brought out?"

"Oooh, almond," the young man said. "Maybe I should get a hazelnut latte then."

Spaz drifted over to the box of little wax paper sheets while Maggie quietly died inside.

"Quit twitching," Wyatt muttered. "It encourages him."

"I'm not twitching," Maggie snapped back, flicking her thumbnails with her fingers.

"Oh look, baby!" the young woman squeaked.

Her friend looked up from his phone. He was probably already posting his Yelp review. "What?"

"Look at these handmade coffee mugs," she said, and Maggie didn't pick one up and beat her with it.

"Yeah, those are made locally, right down the street," Kirk said, the ambassador of the Shop Small movement in Apalach.

"I guess I am going to go ahead and get the vanilla chai latte, decaf, with soy if you have it," the man said. He looked at his wife or girlfriend. "Honey?"

She put the coffee mug down and smiled cheerfully. "I'll keep it simple," she said, and turned to Kirk. "May I please have the café au lait, half skim and half soy, with four raw sugars?"

"Sure thing," Kirk said helpfully.

He turned his attention to the immense, complicated-looking, ten-million-dollar metal sculpture that he called The Big Sexy Machine. "Oh, look," he said almost brightly. "Here's Spaz."

Spaz wasn't actually there, but he was approaching at a flat-out meander, truffle in hand.

Four and a half minutes later, the young couple finally turned away from the espresso counter, dragging their smelly coffees under Maggie's nose, and Maggie stepped up to the counter. Kirk waited, hip kipped out with one fist propped on it, chilling.

Maggie opened her mouth, but Wyatt put a finger to her lips and leaned around her. "Let me just order my coffee before you piss him off."

"Have you thought about coming in ten minutes ahead of her?" Kirk asked.

"I have," Wyatt said. "I'd like a latte, no fancy stuff, any way you want to make it."

"Wyatt—" Maggie started indignantly.

"Hush. Just let me get my latte and then you can violate his civil rights."

"I see you busted her out of the methadone clinic again," Kirk said.

"*Any* kind," Wyatt said. "*Any* way that you would like to prepare that coffee, because I don't really care what time it is, but for her, it's 2:45."

"It's 2:51," Kirk said drily, pulling two tall paper cups from beside the cash register. "I made your coffees ten minutes ago. And yes, you will get it any way I like, because I made it already."

Maggie stared at Kirk.

"Pretty soon, we'll have you getting all the way to three o'clock without pieces of you falling off your body," he said pleasantly.

Maggie picked up her coffee and drew it close. "Your timing sucks. It's been a really crappy couple of days."

"Hey," he said. "I know it has. I'm really sorry that happened. The skinny guy, right?"

"Yeah," Wyatt said.

Maggie rarely brought Dwight into Kirk's. Dwight didn't understand why Folger's wasn't okay.

"Well, I hope he pulls through," Kirk went on. "But I've been through enough really crappy stuff to know that sometimes a little bit of your normal is what gets you through the really bad days. And the lattes are on the house. Go with God."

Maggie suddenly felt a little contrite.

"Geez, don't give me that human being to human being look," Kirk said. "It gives me the creeps."

He turned away and headed out from behind the counter.

"Hey, Spaz!" he yelled. "Who falls asleep in a coffee shop?"

By the time Maggie and Wyatt got back outside, she'd already had several swallows of her latte, just warmer than lukewarm, exactly how she liked it. Meanwhile, Wyatt tried really hard to get a sip of his, but had to settle for licking the foam since, even after ten minutes, the rest of his coffee was Kirk's usual lava-degrees.

They had just walked over to Maggie's Jeep when her phone buzzed. She set her cup down on the hood, pulled out her phone and answered without looking.

"Maggie Hamilton," she said.

"Maggie, it's Arthur Shultz," Dwight's father replied.

Maggie's heart started beating a little faster. "Is he out of surgery?" she asked.

"Yes. They finished about forty-five minutes ago, and he's back in ICU."

"Is that bad?"

"No, they just want to keep him there for now," Arthur said. "They've gotta watch him really good for blood clots and his blood pressure."

"Okay," Maggie said, trying not to feel too safe. "How did the surgery go? Did they say anything about his spinal injury?"

"They don't know for sure, yet. They got the bullet, and they repaired one of his vertebra, but it's the nerve they're worried about. They don't know if he's gonna walk, Maggie. They gotta wait till the swelling goes down inside."

Maggie heard Arthur's voice break, and her heart hurt for him. Arthur Shultz was one of the nicest men she knew. Dwight had three sisters and a brother, all of them just as hyper and nervous as he was, and Maggie had never heard his father raise his voice to any of them. Dwight's mother Phyllis was a tiny little wrecking ball that terrified anyone who was in trouble, but Arthur got mad about twice a year.

"When? Do they know when they'll have some idea?" she asked.

"They said we need to give it about forty-eight hours and they might know something more solid," Arthur answered. He sounded so weary. "Till then, we lift him up, you hear me, girl?"

"Yes, sir." She blinked back tears for someone else's pain and goodness. "We will. How's Amy?"

"That little girl's the toughest thing on two feet. She's doing all right. They're letting her sleep in the empty room next to his for a few hours."

"Okay." Maggie looked up at Wyatt, who had been looming over her shoulder, listening in. "Thank you, Arthur."

"You find the boy yet?"

"Not yet."

"Well, you go take care of all that," Arthur said. "We'll take care of Dwight."

"Yes, sir."

Arthur hung up and Maggie leaned against the Jeep and let out a breath she felt like she'd been holding for hours. Wyatt set his coffee down on a nearby bench and vigorously rubbed at his face with both hands. Then he stood there for a moment, staring down at the sidewalk, before picking up his coffee and walking back to her.

"I'm going to this press conference," he said. "What are you doing?"

"I'm going to go back to driving around, looking for a needle."

Wyatt put a hand to the back of her head, pulled her toward him, and kissed her forehead, his mouth lingering there for a moment. "It's good. He'll be good," he said into her skin.

Maggie nodded, and watched Wyatt as he got into his truck and headed toward the bridge at the end of Market. Then she grabbed her coffee and climbed into the Jeep.

Once she got her windows down, she pulled out, made a left, and drove the two blocks down Avenue D to Water Street, which ran along Scipio Creek. Ahead of her was her favorite place in Apalach, Riverfront Park. It was just a small patch of grass with some benches, a fountain, and a few shrimp boats tied up at the day dock, but Maggie had always liked being there.

For a long time, she had lost the park. She'd watched her ex-husband die right out there on the creek, which opened up into the bay and the Gulf beyond. It had been months before she could come back. Now it was hers again, and she took a deep breath, drinking in the damp, salty air.

She looked down Water Street as a car pulled up behind her and waited. She decided to make a left, toward Boudreaux's Sea-Fair, Scipio Creek Marina, and the Water Street Hotel at the far end.

Next to Boudreaux's two large buildings was an old brick building that had been a cotton warehouse at one time, when shipping cotton had been a huge industry in Apalach. Now it was derelict and boarded up, a waste of history and a waterfront lot. Maggie pulled the Jeep over, parked it in the patch of oyster shells and weeds that passed for a parking area, and got out of the Jeep.

Boudreaux had owned this place at one time but sold it without developing it. She didn't know who bought it, or how many times it had changed hands, but no one had ever done anything with it.

It was big and dark and no one ever went in there. It was as good a place as any for two people to go unnoticed, although Maggie didn't see Adrian Nichols' 1996 Honda anywhere. Who knew if they even had it anymore.

The last time Maggie had been over here, a half-door in back near the old loading dock had been falling off its hinges. She walked through the weeds and tall grass, watching out for the broken bottles that sometimes ended up over there, tossed by underage kids sneaking beers or customers of the small pub across the street.

The door was still unrepaired, and Maggie pulled it out as far as she could, hunched down, and slid inside. She stood, turned on the flashlight app on her phone, and pointed it around the cavernous room. The dust on the floor was thick and undisturbed, the wooden staircase half-crumbled and ruling out anyone upstairs. They weren't there. It had been a long shot.

She ducked back outside, squinting and blinking against the bright, late afternoon sun, then pulled the door shut the best she could. She stood up, wiped a few cobwebs from her jeans, and walked back around to the front.

She stood by the Jeep, looking down the street toward the marina, and decided it wouldn't hurt to look at a few of the closed-up shopfronts that faced the water. In the 19th and early 20th centuries, Water Street had been a very lively thoroughfare, facing the creek as it did, with all of the boats bringing in cotton and sponges and other goods, and larger boats loading them up to take them north. Now, many of the waterfront shops were closed up, slowly being bought, remodeled, and added to Apalach's charming and trendy downtown. For now, they were empty and could possibly be a good place to lay low.

She was about to get into the Jeep when she heard someone raise his voice.

"Hey!" he called from across the street.

Maggie turned to see Adrian Nichols' father standing outside the pub, smoking. He tossed the cigarette butt down on the sidewalk and started crossing the road. She didn't know him well enough to be sure he was drunk, but he wasn't sober. She reflexively touched her holster, felt the uneven texture of her grip, then walked to the edge of the grass.

"You're the lady cop," he said loudly. "The one from this morning."

"Can I help you?"

Maggie glanced past him when she saw movement in the corner of her eye. A burly man wearing well-worn white rubber boots, official footwear of the seafood industry, had come to stand in the doorway, and was squinting against the sun.

"Yeah, you can help me," Nichols said with a touch of a slur. "Why don't you get out there and look for my kid instead of looking at real estate?"

"I am looking for your son, Mr. Nichols."

Two more men stepped to the doorway of the pub, and the first man made room by stepping out onto the sidewalk.

"I don't see you people doin' anything but waiting for the TV people and feeling sorry for the poor little bullied boy who can't take care of himself."

Nichols had made his way to her and stood just a couple of feet away in the road. Close enough to be confrontational, not close enough to be illegal. Reflexively, Maggie loosened her limbs, balanced her weight between both feet.

"Mr. Nichols, the Sheriff's Office and the Apalach PD are spending all of their time and manpower on finding both boys," she said. She spoke firmly and without fear. With many of these guys, that was enough, their particular aggressiveness preferring the path of least resistance. With others, it wasn't that easy. She didn't know which one he was.

But she did know a couple of the guys that were standing in front of the pub, and they knew her. Nichols might be a shrimper, but he wasn't yet a local. She wasn't very worried about having to deal with the man in broad daylight.

"All I'm hearing about is how in this little podunk town, can't any cops find either one of these high school kids," the man said. She could smell the beer on his breath, most likely not any of the artisanal micro-brews the tourists were drinking two blocks away.

Maggie cut her eyes quickly to the left, as she saw two cars turn onto Water Street back down by Boudreaux's, then looked quickly back at Nichols.

"Sir, I think it's time for you to go home."

⚓ ⚓ ⚓

Bennett Boudreaux saw Maggie's Jeep first, parked out in front of the old Crawford building. He registered the few men in front of the pub, and that Maggie was speaking with someone before he was in his parking lot and his view was blocked.

He shut off his Mercedes, got out of the car, and decided to walk down and see what was going on. Most likely, a couple of the shrimpers had had a few before work, or a couple of the oystermen had had a few after. It wasn't common for fights to break out in the local places, but it wasn't shocking when they did, either.

He walked back out to Water Street and headed up the block, sliding his keys into his right pants pocket. He felt as much as heard the quiet metallic clicking as they landed against the switchblade he'd carried since he was a boy.

He could see now that the man Maggie was talking to was Victor Nichols, the father of the missing boy. He knew Nichols; he bought his loads of shrimp from him, when he actually went out and caught some. The man worked erratically and often smelled of alcohol when bringing his trawler in first thing in the morning.

Boudreaux was a short block away when he saw the man reach out and jab a finger into Maggie's shoulder. Before the flash of anger had even announced itself to Boudreaux's system, Maggie had grabbed the man's hand with one of hers, twisted him down and around, put her other hand behind his shoulder, and pressed him down to a crouch.

Boudreaux sighed, flicking his thumbnail against the shaft of the switchblade as he continued walking.

⚓ ⚓ ⚓

"I said 'Okay'!" Nichols yelled, kneeling in the gravel beside the road.

Maggie twisted his thumb back just a little bit further as she pressed against his shoulder with her other hand. "I'd like you to lie down on your stomach, Mr. Nichols," she said.

"Take it easy!"

"I am taking it easy, sir," she said quietly. "I need you to lie down on your stomach."

She assisted him in that regard, and once he was on his stomach, she let go of his shoulder and pressed her knee into the small of his back. "Both hands behind your back, please."

"Y'all want some help, there, Maggie?" one of the fishermen called from the middle of the road.

"That's okay," she called back. "Thank you though. Your hand, sir."

"You've got my thumb!"

"Your other hand," she said with a sigh.

He brought his other arm around back. She put one of the cuffs on it, then cuffed the other as she released his thumb. She stood up, noticing as she did, that Boudreaux was approaching. She sighed again and looked down at Mr. Nichols as she pulled out her phone.

"I didn't do anything!" Nichols snapped, managing to whine at the same time.

"Sir, it's against the law for you to put your hands on a law enforcement officer," she said as she thumbed through her contacts and tapped the non-emergency line for Apalach PD. "I believe you're also intoxicated."

"My son is missing!" he barked indignantly.

"Well, he's not in the bar," she answered.

A male voice answered the phone. "Apalachicola Police Department. This is Sgt. Bryce. May I help you?"

"Hey, Alan. It's Maggie Hamilton."

"Hey, Maggie, what's up?"

"I have somebody who needs to be taken in. Public intoxication and we'll see how we feel about assaulting an officer. I can't do it. Can you send somebody over to the old Crawford building on Water Street?"

"Yeah, sure," Bryce answered. "Lon's over at Hole in the Wall grabbing our lunch."

"Thanks," Maggie said.

"No problem."

Maggie disconnected. The Hole in the Wall Raw Bar was just around the corner on Avenue D.

She looked up at Boudreaux. "Hello, Mr. Boudreaux."

"Hello, Maggie," he said pleasantly. "What's taking place here in the road on such a nice afternoon?"

"It's nothing," Maggie said. "Timewasting."

She reached down and grabbed Nichols by her cuffs. "Let's get up on our feet, Mr. Nichols."

She helped him to stand and looked down the street as she saw an Apalach PD cruiser round the corner at a leisurely pace. She wiped some dirt from her hands as Sgt. Lon Woodman pulled abreast of her and stopped in the road.

"Hey, Maggie, what's shaking?" Lon asked with a smile, chewing on a grouper finger.

Lon was a handsome, African-American man who had touches of white at the temples, despite being the same age as Maggie. He'd played on the baseball team with David all through junior high and high school.

"Hey, Lon."

"Hey, Lon!" two of the oystermen called, smiling and waving.

"Hey, y'all, what's up?" he answered, waving out his window.

He shut the cruiser down and unfolded from the driver's seat. He was almost as tall as Wyatt, but lanky, and while Wyatt loped like a happy giraffe, Lon oozed gracefully.

He came around the front of his cruiser. "Dwight came outa surgery a little while ago. You hear?"

"Yeah." Maggie nodded. "Arthur called."

"So what's this guy's deal?"

"He's Adrian Nichols' dad," Maggie said. "Got a little worked up."

"Assault?"

Maggie shrugged. "Not much of one. Public intoxication? I just don't have time and I need him out of my hair."

"That's cool, that's cool," he said. "I'll take him in and let Todd bore him sober."

Maggie looked over at Nichols, who was sneering at Lon. Great. Apparently, he didn't like *black* cops, either. That should be entertaining for Lon.

Lon quickly read Nichols his rights, and Maggie nodded goodbye to Boudreaux and pulled away.

⚓   ⚓   ⚓

Lon walked Nichols over to the cruiser, opened the back-passenger door, and tried to guide him in. Nichols weaved a bit.

"Come on, get it together," Lon said. "My fish getting cold, man."

He got Nichols in, slammed the door, and got back in the driver's seat. Boudreaux walked up to the back window and tapped, as Lon started up the car.

Lon looked over his shoulder and buzzed the window down. Boudreaux calmly peered down at Nichols.

"Don't bring your shrimp to my docks anymore," he said quietly.

"What?! I barely had two beers," the man protested.

Boudreaux bent at the waist so Nichols could hear him better. "Any man who raises his hand to a woman should have his head displayed on a pike for all of the other villagers to see," he said calmly. "Take your shrimp somewhere else."

He turned and headed back the way he'd come, as Lon rolled the window back up.

"What the hell, man," Nichols grumbled.

"Man, you even know who you're talkin' to?" Lon asked, shaking his head.

"Yeah, Boudreaux. Some kinda big-time badass. Looks like another middle-aged rich guy to me."

Lon laughed. "That was his daughter, man." He put the car in gear. "I was you, I'd praise God, take my little shrimps, and go."

CHAPTER
FOURTEEN

Wyatt turned on the faucet, and looked in the men's room mirror as he washed his hands. His brown, wavy hair could use a trim, and so could his mustache, now that he noticed. He nodded at Quincy as the deputy came in to use the facilities.

Wyatt finished washing his hands, took off his SO ball cap, and ran a little water through his hair to try to smooth it down or something. He was giving his mustache the same treatment when Quincy came to the sink next to him to wash up. Quincy looked at him in the mirror and smiled.

"You got a couple nose hairs, too." He smiled as Wyatt gave him a look. "You want me to pluck 'em out for ya? I do it for my wife all the time."

"Shut up, Quincy," Wyatt said. He turned off the water and turned on the hot air dryer, stuck his hands underneath it.

"Bledsoe's looking for you," Quincy said. "Lotta press out there."

"I saw them."

"You want some irony?"

"Oh, sure," Wyatt said. "I never have enough of *that*."

Quincy joined him at the dryer. "Well, when you were Sheriff, we didn't even have a Public Information Officer anymore, 'cause the press all wanted you, anyway," he said. "Now, you're the Public Information Officer, and you're still stuck with the press."

"Oh, I don't know," Wyatt said. "Bledsoe really enjoys a good photo opp."

"Whatever. Guy's a piece of work."

Wyatt shrugged. "He did a good thing for Dwight and Amy."

Quincy nodded. "Yeah, all right, I'll give you that, but I have yet to see him put on a vest, you know what I'm saying? You never sent us anyplace that you weren't going into first. He sends us all out of here like we're delivering pizzas, and he hides behind his desk."

Wyatt nodded. This was something he heard a lot, not that he hadn't already made note of it.

"I gotta get out front, Quincy," he said. "Let's see if the mother can get this kid to come in."

He pushed through the bathroom door, walked down the hall, and found Ginny Warner where he'd left her, sitting stiff-backed in the lobby, staring out the window at the cluster of reporters and cameramen who were stationed at the foot of the wide steps.

"Mrs. Warner? Are you ready to go on out?" he asked gently.

She nodded. "Yes."

He opened the door for her, then followed her out as the reporters all came to attention and jockeyed for better position. He put a hand on Ginny's shoulder and moved her to stand just behind and beside him. Then he gave the press a minute to situate themselves before speaking.

"I'm not going to be taking any questions today, so please be aware of that up front," he said. "We're here to give the public an update on our search for Ryan Warner and Adrian Nichols, and to allow Ryan's mother to try to speak to her son and help him to understand that the best thing for everyone is for him to contact us and arrange to turn himself in." He looked around the group. "If you're going to edit something out, please edit me, okay?"

He cleared his throat and went on.

"We are currently following up on leads that we're hoping will help us to locate these two boys, and to bring them home safely. Both of them," he added, looking directly at one of the cameras. "I want to remind the people watching that, while we do believe that the shooting of Deputy Dwight Shultz was unintentional, we also believe that Ryan Warner is still armed. If you see him, please don't interact with him. Just call 911, the Sheriff's Office, or the Apalach PD. Those numbers should be on your screens."

He cleared his throat and wished for the Mountain Dew that was sweating on his desk. It was a thousand degrees with 200% humidity.

"At this time, I'll let Ryan's mother, Ginny Warner, say a few words."

He turned, put a hand on the small of her back, and guided her forward. She looked scared to death, and he felt badly about that.

She swallowed a couple of times, then looked into the cameras that were pointed at her.

"I know that a terrible thing has happened, and that my son has taken actions that have—I'm very, very sorry for the pain and fear that this deputy's family are going through right now. But I hope that you will believe me when I say that Ryan has never wanted to hurt anyone in his life. He acted on impulse, when he was not in his normal frame of mind, and I know in my heart that he regrets it so deeply. I also know that he's frightened and confused and doesn't know what to do to end all of this now."

A tear ran down her right cheek. "Last year, when we first moved here, it was the middle of turtle season. Ryan loves animals. He wants to be a vet, and he couldn't wait to go through the volunteer training. One day, when he was helping an adult volunteer check on the nests in their section, a big group of kids came by. It was a family reunion, and there were several kids from about four on up to twelve, and they were watching from outside the barrier, and asking questions. I watched Ryan spend over an hour answering their questions, and teaching them why it was so important to not leave holes on the beach, or to litter."

She looked down for a moment, wiped her mouth, then looked back up. "He talked about that for days, how much fun it was to share the turtles with the kids, and he even thought maybe he'd be a biology teacher if he didn't get to go to vet school."

She cleared her throat, and Wyatt cleared his reflexively.

"That's what kind of person Ryan really is," she went on quietly. "What happened Friday, that's not Ryan. Ryan, I know you didn't mean for this to happen. I know you're scared. But please, please. Please call me, or the Sheriff's Office. Please let Adrian Nichols go home. And you come home, too. We will get through this together, I promise. But you have to do the right thing now."

She turned and looked over her shoulder at Wyatt. He stepped forward as several reporters started shooting questions out.

"No questions," he said quietly. "Let us just get back to work resolving this situation."

The bridge out to SGI, or St. George Island, was one of Maggie's favorite locations in Franklin County. She didn't get out to the island nearly as often as she would have liked, especially now that the kids were bigger and weren't begging for rides to the beach. Given a preference, she wouldn't drive over there much at all during the months of June and July, because the tourist traffic, as mild as she knew it was, was just a little too much for her.

Even though it was June now, she felt a sense of relief and space the moment she pulled onto the four-mile bridge. The water was calm this afternoon, and the sun glinted off it like someone had dumped a shipping container of diamonds into the bay. She watched the gray and brown pelicans hang-gliding over the water to her left, and on her right, a large group of seagulls followed a shrimp boat that was heading out for the night.

When the old bridge to the island had become badly damaged, the Eastpoint and island ends had been repurposed into long fishing piers that were always popular with the locals, but were now also covered with summertime visitors.

Maggie rolled down her windows, breathed in the salt air, and was surprised by the squawk of a pelican as it coasted alongside the driver's side a moment, just off the bridge, then divebombed whatever prey it had spotted down on the water, just below the surface.

A few minutes later, the bridge became the road, and Maggie stopped at the stop sign on Gulf Beach

Drive. There was no one else at the intersection at the moment, and she tapped her nails against the steering wheel as she decided which way to go first. She had no definite destination, just a weary hope that she could roam around and accidentally find Ryan Warner. His mother said he loved the island, and she'd run out of more likely places to look.

The one thing the island did have, if someone was trying to stay unseen, was a lot of empty houses that people weren't in at the moment, and a lot of out of town vehicles belonging to the people who *were* there. The former might be an attractive place to hide, though the chances of discovery were good. The latter provided decent camouflage for a car that every cop in the county was seeking.

Maggie decided she'd go left, east toward the state park end of the island. The boys weren't in the park, not in a car, anyway. Patrol cars went through it three times a day, and the rangers were keeping a lookout as well. But the houses between Maggie and the park were vacation rentals, many of them rented weekly, and it would be easier to avoid sticking out in one of them.

On the west end, there was the traffic and confusion of the public beaches in which to hide, but the houses were mainly second homes and longer-term, high-end rentals. They terminated in a gated community that wouldn't exactly be ideal.

It was slow going along Gulf Breeze, what with people in golf carts, people on bikes, and small groups of people with pool noodles and floats and buckets and coolers and overheated toddlers growing out of their bodies. That was okay with Maggie; it forced her to go slowly and look at each house she passed. With some of the empty ones, she drove through driveways and around the back. With others, it was clear that families were staying there.

It took her twenty minutes to get to the entrance of the state park, where she turned around, and pulled into one of the parking spaces at a small pull-off. These spots were for people looking to do a little shore fishing, or those who preferred the company of egrets to the company of a thousand people from the Midwest. Maggie got out to stretch her legs. A break in the sea oats provided a sandy path to the beach. Maggie walked past the sign warning about rip-currents and the lack of lifeguards, and walked onto the beach.

After the broodiness of the weather the last couple of days, it was surprising to see the surf so calm. People bent at the waist like obedient servants, searching for shells, and down the beach a man stood next to a cooler, his line cast just off the shore break. Behind him, a stately heron kept him company, hoping to assist him with his catch.

Maggie took in a deep breath, then blew it out. It was time to head to the other end of the island, just so she could tell herself she checked. She knew she was reaching. She didn't have a lot of hope that Ryan and Adrian were on the island.

Her phone buzzed in her pocket, and she pulled it out.

"Maggie Hamilton."

"Hey, Maggie, it's Myles."

He sounded a little excited, so she went ahead and started walking back toward the car.

"Hey. What's up?" she asked.

"Ryan Warner just did a Facebook Live," he answered.

"Wait. He's live on Facebook right now?" Maggie started walking faster.

"No, he *was* live about thirty minutes ago," he answered. "We didn't hear about it until it was already over. We're getting ready to look at it now."

"You can still watch it?"

"Yeah, the video stays up, it's just not live anymore."

"Okay, I get it." She hit the asphalt and hurried to her car. "I'll be there in fifteen minutes."

CHAPTER
FIFTEEN

She was there in eleven. When she hurried down the hall, she found Wyatt, Quincy, and Bledsoe hovering behind Myles, who was seated at the conference table with his personal laptop. Wyatt looked over his shoulder as she came in.

"Hey, we're getting ready to watch it again. Come here."

"What's he doing?" Maggie asked.

"Just talking, really," Wyatt answered.

"Is Adrian in it, too?"

"We don't see Adrian anywhere on camera, but you do hear him at the end, so he's alive. Restrained, maybe."

Maggie went to stand beside him. Myles looked over his shoulder at her.

"Okay," he said. He already had Ryan Warner's Facebook page up. The live post was at the top. The still picture showed another close-up shot of Ryan. He was wearing a blue t-shirt.

"He took off the hoodie," Maggie said. "Or he got fresh clothes somewhere."

"I checked the YouTube video," Quincy said. "You can see the collar of this shirt sticking up from the hoodie in that one. I think he just took it off."

"Okay." Maggie wondered if he was someplace air-conditioned. A heavy hoodie in this heat was unthinkable.

"You guys ready?" Myles asked, sounding a little irritated. They were all on edge after four days; no one took it personally.

He clicked on the post, and Ryan immediately started speaking.

"Um, this is Ryan Warner," he said, sounding old and weary. "I'm making this live post because I want to tell the family of the deputy I shot—Deputy Shultz—I want to tell them that I'm really sorry."

He swiped at his forehead with the back of his hand, and Maggie decided he was probably without AC.

"I know I took a gun on the bus—to school—and I know that was crazy and wrong. I can't really explain what I was thinking. I didn't even know what I wanted to do with it, except that I wanted to scare Adrian and Stuart and them."

He sighed and leaned just a little to reach off-camera. When he did, there was something about his face from that angle, something about his partial profile, that made him look much younger than seventeen. Certainly, Ginny Warner had seen this by now. She'd probably watched it a dozen times already, just to see him, and hear his voice.

Maggie wondered if his profile struck her the same way; if she saw her seven-year-old son or her ten-year-old son when she looked at him from the side. Her twelve-year-old son, who hadn't yet picked up a loaded gun and shoved it underneath his hoodie.

He straightened back up and brought a half-empty bottle of water to his lips, took a drink. Maggie wondered where he got it.

"I wonder if we should look at security camera footage from the gas stations and mini-marts," she thought out loud.

Myles clicked the video to stop it. "That wouldn't be such a bad idea if there weren't so many of them."

"Plus, you're talking about let's say fifteen places, times four days," Quincy said.

"Yeah, we don't have the manpower for it," Bledsoe said. "And it would only tell us where he had been, not where he is."

"But it would probably put us in the right neighborhood," Wyatt said, thinking

"Yeah, probably."

"But you're right, we don't have the manpower, or the time if we did," Wyatt conceded. "Every twenty-four hours gives us another twenty-four hours of video to watch."

"Well, maybe what we should do is go to each gas station or convenience store or whatever and show them pictures of these boys," Maggie said. "Just because they sell the paper doesn't mean they read it. Somebody might remember him."

"Look, if we can't find this kid in the next twelve hours or so, then, yeah," Bledsoe said. "We'll use some of our hours doing that. But for all we know he got that water out of Adrian's car or something. I don't think we divert too many of our resources that way yet. I'll see if I can squeeze a couple of guys in for it."

"Okay, sorry, just thinking out loud," Maggie said. "Go ahead, Myles."

Myles turned the video back on, and Maggie heard Ryan swallow a big gulp of water. As he put it down, the screen started scrolling and flashing beneath him. Maggie couldn't see it that well standing up.

"What is all that?"

"Comments," Myles said. "People can comment live, too."

"Okay."

"I'm wondering why he did the Facebook thing instead of another YouTube video," Wyatt said.

"I have a theory," Myles said. "Because I was wondering that when Quincy said there was a video on his page." He looked at Maggie. "We've had his Facebook up on here since Friday, over in the bullpen, but other than posts from some of his friends in Orlando, there hasn't been anything going on."

"So what's your theory?" Bledsoe asked a little impatiently.

"Faster upload. YouTube videos are a pain to upload, especially if you're on your phone. He's gotta be in a hurry, right, because he keeps his phone turned off so he can't get tracked."

"Can you make it full screen?" Bledsoe asked. "Let's see if we can pick anything out of the background there."

"Yeah, but it's not really full screen, the way Netflix would be. It's better, though," he said, clicking the little icon.

It did make it larger, but not by much. The bigger problem was that it was fairly dark.

"I don't think he has any lights on," Quincy said, mirroring her own thought. "That could be something. He might be somewhere without electric."

"He could just have them off," Bledsoe mused.

"It was kinda dark in the YouTube video, too, though," Myles said. "I think Quince might be right."

"Hold on," Wyatt said. "If he's someplace without electricity, how's he keeping his phone charged? Kyle has to charge his phone something like ten times a day."

"He has it off a lot, though," Maggie said. "I mean, we haven't been able to pick him up at all, except for when he first left the scene."

"Adrian's car," Quincy piped up. "I don't know any kid with a car who doesn't have a car charger in there. These guys can't handle the idea of their phone going dead."

"Good point," Bledsoe said. "Let's get this going again, please."

Myles clicked it back on.

"I know probably nobody will believe me," Ryan said. "Or care, actually, whether it's true. I get it. I get why people are really, really angry. But I'm telling the truth."

He glanced just past the camera, off at an angle. Then he reached over with his free hand and pulled something toward him. It looked like he was at a counter or a work table. The object didn't come into view, but it sounded substantial. To Maggie, it sounded like it could well be a handgun.

He stood up, picked up the phone in one hand, and the object with the other, but that arm remained at his side, and they couldn't see what he was holding. He walked a few steps, still holding the phone, though it kipped a little diagonally, leaned over like he was looking at something, then walked back and sat down.

"Can you stop it?" Wyatt asked quickly. Myles did. Ryan sat there with his mouth open, the picture blurred.

"Did you hear that, when he was walking?"

"Sounded like leaves, papers," Myles said, nodding.

"Trash," Wyatt said. "If you back it up a second when he got up? You can just see some graffiti on the wall. Not the one behind him, the one to his left."

"Let me rewind," Myles said, and dragged the little icon backward on the white line. He clicked it to play.

"I know probably nobody will believe me," Ryan was again saying. "Or care, actually, whether it's true. I get it. I get why people are really, really angry. But I'm telling the truth."

They watched him stand up, then pick up the phone and what Maggie assumed was the gun. He took a few steps and leaned, and they could just see the portion of a wall that Wyatt meant, covered with graffiti. The only thing Maggie could make out for sure was a four-letter word in giant red letters. Then it was out of view again.

"Looks like an abandoned building of some kind," Myles said. "Too bad we have a crap-ton of those in this county."

Ryan sat back down. "I also want to say, Mom, I'm really sorry about all of this. I'm so sorry. I didn't mean it. I wish we could just—"

"Somebody get me the hell out of here!!" they heard Adrian Nichols yell angrily, and Ryan reached out and turned off the camera.

Everybody in the room either took a deep breath or let one out.

"Okay, we think he's in an abandoned building, maybe a house, maybe a storage place, something, but abandoned building is sounding good," Wyatt said.

"Yeah," Quincy agreed. "Probably. We don't know about the first video, but this one, yeah."

"You should see all the crap these people are saying on the comments," Myles said. "You'd think it would be distracting, but I don't think he was even looking at them. Usually, you know, it's kind of an interactive thing; the person is answering questions as they're asked, saying hi, whatever."

"So what are they saying?" Maggie asked.

"Oh, it's nice," Myles said, reaching for his wireless mouse again. "Here."

The video started going again.

"Um, this is Ryan Warner. I'm making this live post because I want to tell the family of the deputy I shot—Deputy Shultz—I want to tell them that I'm really sorry."

The comments started scrolling almost immediately.

"It's hard to see," Maggie said.

Myles started reading the comments as they scrolled up. "*Loser. Hey, Ryan*, happy face, *go Ryan*, sad face, *go shoot yourself*, praying hands, okay, I won't read that one out loud. *Just call someone*. More praying hands. Oh, look, it's Newman. He has laughing faces. Myles turned around. "There's like two hundred that came in while he was live, and they're still posting."

"That's nuts," Maggie said. She leaned in. "What's that one?"

It was an ad for a suicide hotline. Wonderful. She watched as Myles went back to scrolling. The comments were all scrolling so fast, and the thing that caught her eye didn't register in her brain until it passed.

"Stop, go up," she said, leaning closer.

"What is it?" Wyatt asked.

"I don't know," she said. "Something looked familiar or something."

Myles scrolled for just a second, and Maggie reflexively reached out and snatched the mouse, stopped the comments.

"Which—" Myles started, then he saw it.

Maggie was simply startled at first when she saw the name and familiar tiny picture. But the message made her want to throw up.

"Is that your Sky?" Quincy asked.

Maggie straightened up as Wyatt leaned down to read, but Maggie already knew what the comment said.

Ryan, I know where you are. I'm coming to talk to you.

SIXTEEN

Ordinarily, Maggie didn't speed on the bridge between Eastpoint and Apalach. There were too many tourists gawking as they drove on the two-lane bridge, and too many pelicans and seagulls miscalculating their altitude or stopping for a quick break. Today, however, Maggie's Jeep ran twenty miles over the speed limit of thirty-five, and her mind twenty miles an hour over that.

As Wyatt and the other guys watched, Maggie had tried to call Sky, gotten her voice mail, and left a short message to call her back. Myles hurriedly tried to get a ping on the phone, and did manage to get a ping on the tower closest to Maggie's house.

She'd tried to use Find My Phone to get her location, but by then Sky's phone was turned off. She knew Kyle was at his friend Shayne's house, so he wouldn't be able to tell her if Sky was home. In the hope that she was, and in the absence of anything else that would satisfy her urge to take some kind of physical action, Maggie had decided to go to the house herself.

Meanwhile, Myles and Wyatt were going through Ryan's Facebook posts, further back than they had before, to see if there were any interactions between Ryan and Sky. Sky had said she didn't really know the boy, but she'd seen the video because she'd been on his Friends list.

Her mind whirled with questions about whether Sky had been dishonest with her, and why she would do something so stupid as to try to find Ryan Warner. She was a cop's kid. She wasn't naïve or ignorant. She knew a bad situation when she saw one. Maggie couldn't help wondering, over and over, why she would do this. In her mind, the question came out as *Why would you do this to me, Sky?* even though that question made her ashamed.

Once she got off the bridge and onto 98, she started reasoning with herself. Sky would be at the house. She would have rethought what she'd said to Ryan, realized what a bad idea her impulsive comment was. She wouldn't put herself in danger that way, especially for a kid she barely knew. She barely knew him, right? The idea that maybe he was someone important to Sky, someone she would do something stupid for, made Maggie want to throw up.

Maggie took several deep breaths as she drove the last couple of miles to her house. Sky would be there.

She had reconsidered, knew she couldn't actually go to this kid. *How did she know where he was? How?*

She should have called Maggie if she knew where the boys were. She was probably thinking about that right now, making sure it was the right thing to do. She was thinking about that, and she'd forgotten to turn her phone back on. Or it was just dead.

When Maggie stopped in the road, waiting for traffic to let her turn into her driveway, her heart stopped pounding and felt like it stopped beating altogether. Sky's truck wasn't in the driveway.

The rational part of Maggie's mind knew that this meant Sky wasn't where Maggie needed her to be. The other part, the part where every cell of her motherhood dwelled, was going to look anyway. She'd look anyway, the way a desperate person looks in the freezer for their keys, even though they know they wouldn't have put them there.

There was a slight gap in traffic, and Maggie whipped out in front of a blue mini-van that she could still hear honking after it had passed behind her. White dust flew up from the crushed oyster shell driveway and Maggie sped up to the house. It was only once she'd slammed to a stop that she realized she had forgotten to watch out for Coco, and some part of her heart registered shame and guilt, but Coco wasn't outside, and that was a good thing, but another bad sign.

Maggie left the Jeep door open behind her as she ran up the porch steps. She heard Coco dancing and keening on the other side of the front door as she jerkily shoved the key in the dead bolt. Then she flung the door open, barely missing Stoopid.

She could feel the emptiness of the house as soon as she ran in. The lack of any of her people.

"Sky?" she called anyway. "Kyle?"

She ran down the hall toward the bedrooms, Coco and Stoopid on her heels. Kyle's door was open, his bed kind of made, his pajama bottoms on the floor where he'd dropped them that morning. She glanced at them for just a second, then ducked back out to Sky's room.

When she opened the door, she saw her daughter's battered brown leather backpack, a gift from three years ago, lying on her bed. It was accompanied by piles of notebooks and papers, an open differential equations textbook, and a make-up bag full of pens and pencils and highlighters.

Hoping that Sky might have written something down, maybe even doodled Ryan's location, Maggie tore through the loose papers and then flipped through the notebooks, but there was nothing there but math problems and Western Civ notes and several pages of the valedictorian speech Sky was working on. She'd written, read to Maggie, and then rejected every draft.

Seeing her daughter's handwriting was like hearing her voice, and Maggie ignored the hitch in her throat.

She would not cry. She would not pick up Sky's turquoise bandana and sniff her scent like a mother chimp already in mourning. She was a cop, and she would think like a cop. Thinking like a mother would kill any chance she had of finding her daughter. Thinking like a mother would leave her crying in a corner, depending on the men in her life to rescue and return her baby girl. She was not going to be that.

She stalked out of Sky's room, shoved Coco and Stoopid back out of the doorway, and ran to the kitchen. It was the habit of everyone in the household to leave notes on the kitchen island. If a note was required, it was left there. Maggie allowed the quickening of hope that Sky would not go to Ryan without leaving Maggie a note, telling her where to find both of them.

But there was nothing on the island that would help Maggie. The gallon sized canning jar full of utensils was next to the fruit bowl. The crumbs from Kyle's morning toast were on the cutting board. Wyatt had put the mail there last night, and neither one of them had opened it.

Sky had gone to do something stupid and dangerous and had not left Maggie the means to keep her from it.

She pulled her phone from the back pocket of her cargo pants and tapped Sky's number. It went straight to voice mail, but she couldn't hang up, not while she could hear her daughter's voice.

"Hey, this is Sky," it said, with the faint strains of a Third Day song in the background. "I'm either sleeping, studying or ignoring you. Or I'm in class and you should know that and you shouldn't be calling me." Maggie heard the smile in her voice. "If you need me to call you back, leave a message. If this is a telemarketer, go away. I'm a kid and I don't have a job." Her voice turned slightly softer. "If this is my mom, yes, I'm wearing my seat belt."

Maggie had heard the message many times. Sky hadn't changed it in two years. But that last line almost did her in. *Yes, this is your mom*, she thought, *and I need you to come back here right now.*

The tone chimed and Maggie took a calming breath. "Sky, I need you to call me or text me right away. Right away, do you understand? Please."

She wanted to say, 'I love you.' They always made sure the last thing they ever said to each other was 'I love you.' Going out the door, going to bed, ending a phone call. Sky and Kyle teased her, because they knew why Maggie insisted. They knew Maggie needed to make sure that it was the last thing they heard from her if something happened. The truth was that it was the last thing she needed to have heard, if something ever happened to *them*, though she only admitted that in the most secret place in her soul.

But saying 'I love you' meant she was scared. That there was a chance something would happen to her daughter.

"I love you," she said, just before the voice mail beeped and cut her off.

She was about to put the phone away when it buzzed in her hand. It was Wyatt.

"Hey."

"Hey. If she was there you would have called me."

"Yes." She heard him let out a slow breath, although he tried to make it silent.

"Okay. So, Quincy got the range on the cell tower that Sky's phone pinged. Yes, it's the same tower we use at the house, but it also covers roughly from just north of the airport to 98 in the south, and from the water department west to The Prado."

"Okay."

"Just remember, please, that she could have been at the house when she pinged off that tower, and she could be in Eastpoint right now."

"I know. But I'm here, and I don't have anywhere else better to look. Are you still trying Find My Phone on your phone?"

"Yes," he answered. "And I will keep trying. Here's what we're putting together here. Myles has Cooper monitoring both Ryan and Sky's Facebook pages—"

"Did you find any posts between them?"

"Not really, Maggie. A few very short posts from Sky the first week of school, pictures of his class schedule, a post about some pep rally, a couple of 'good luck, take care' kind of things. Since then, there have been a few posts of his that she's given a thumbs-up, but that's it."

"So they probably don't know each other any more than she said they did," Maggie said. She felt relief that she didn't have to feel hurt anymore that Sky might have lied. Or feel bad anymore because she suspected it.

"Probably not," Wyatt said.

"But how did she know where he was?"

"I don't know. Something. Myles and Bledsoe are still looking at the Facebook video, trying to see something we missed, something that one of us will recognize."

"That's it? That's all?"

"Of course not," Wyatt said gently.

"I'm sorry."

"We're dividing up the area this tower covers, and we're getting ready to head out. We've got three units from PD, six from our office, and we're working on a chopper to see if we can spot her truck or Adrian's car. We've got a BOLO out on the Toyota, so if she's on the road…"

"Yeah." Maggie took a deep breath and let it out. "Why did she do this, Wyatt?"

She heard him sigh. "I don't know. We'll ask her tonight when we all get home."

Maggie nodded. "Yeah. Okay. I'm—"

Her phone vibrated and she saw a notification that Wyatt had texted her a picture.

"What's this?"

"I drew a circle on the Google map, of the tower range," he said. "We've all got different sections, but you go wherever it is that you're going and just keep in touch, okay?"

"Okay."

"Maggie."

"What?"

"If by some wild chance you find them, you call it in, do you hear me?"

"Yeah."

"Before you get out of your car."

"Yes."

His voice changed to a near-whisper. "I promise you I will choke you by the neck if you go rushing in someplace without calling."

"I know. I will. I love you," she said hurriedly.

"I love you."

She disconnected and was about to slide the phone into her pocket, when she suddenly turned and slammed the fridge with her fist; once, three times, five. "You come back here right *now*!" she yelled.

Maggie shoved the phone in her pocket, turned, and almost tripped over Stoopid, who was uncharacteristically silent. Coco sat behind him, not smiling, her tail thumping slowly. She knew fear when she heard it, especially Maggie's fear.

"Come on, Coco," Maggie said, and Coco jumped to her feet and followed.

CHAPTER
SEVENTEEN

Sky pulled the Toyota into the mixture of grass, weeds, and gravel that made up the yard in front of the derelict trailer.

She didn't know what kind of car Adrian Nichols had, although Mom and Wyatt had been talking about it the other night; she just hadn't paid attention. She supposed it didn't matter anyway; there were no cars there at all.

That didn't mean Ryan wasn't still in there, though. She sat in the truck, listening. The engine was ticking, and the little keychain hanging from the rearview mirror clicked against the back of it. She glanced at it nervously. Like the truck, it had been her dad's. It had been hanging there when he died, and she wasn't touching it unless she was forced to get rid of the truck someday.

It was one of those keychains they sell at photo studios, the ones with the packages of a million wallet-sized pictures. In the sun-faded picture, she was twelve and Kyle was almost seven. Her dad said one time that he kept it because, in it, she hadn't hit puberty yet. In her head, in the part of her mind that was scared, she heard her dad laugh and she wished he was there.

She was impulsive, like her father. She knew that. Everybody knew that. Wyatt said once that she had a tendency to ride off in all directions at once, like Don Quixote. That was true. She'd reached out to Ryan almost without knowing she was going to. He was just so sad, and scared, and she had known all at once where he was. She'd seen the wall, and she'd already been typing before she'd decided to type.

She'd been excited and determined when she'd left the house, and didn't start to get scared until she was almost here. Now she thought about turning her phone on and calling her mom. Or driving back home and then calling her mom.

But if Ryan was still in there, if her message hadn't chased him away, then he'd already seen her. He would run if she pulled out now. Anyway, her adrenaline might be starting to let her down, but her conviction that she should come hadn't changed. The phone would stay off until she was ready to use it.

The door to the old truck squealed as she pushed it open, and she stuck her phone in her back pocket, left the keys in the ignition, and got out.

The trailer was an old singlewide; dirty white with rusted brown trim. An ancient air conditioner hung precariously from one of the front windows, and a broken and flatted kiddie pool languished in the weeds. The front steps were made of pallets, and they weren't from the former owner. Kids had built them, to make it less strenuous to get inside and party.

The trailer had been empty for at least six or seven years. Nothing ever came of the first time someone broke in and blew through a twelve pack, so more people came, and more beer was drunk, and nobody ever fixed the front door.

Even though her truck was loud and she was in plain sight, she closed the door as quietly as she could, then stood and listened. There was nothing on this section of Oyster Road but this trailer and a lot of woods. Across the road, an empty lot was alive with the sounds of cicadas and frogs and crickets, one shift closing down for the day and the other one getting ready to take over for the night.

The woods behind the trailer seemed quieter, like the wildlife over there had stopped to see what she was doing. The windows were mostly boarded up or covered with tattered mini-blinds. She couldn't tell if anyone *inside* was waiting, too. She wanted to text Ryan and ask him if he was there or tell him that she was. But she didn't want to turn her phone on, and she knew he was keeping his off, too.

Suddenly, she heard her Mom's voice in her head; her practical voice. *It's not gonna be any easier five minutes from now, Boo.* Of course, Mom meant the laundry, the homework, the chicken poop, the tetanus shot. Still, it got her moving.

She walked across the yard, her Van's picking up stickers with every step, the weeds dragging themselves across her bare legs, probably depositing ticks on her; ticks she would find in the shower sometime. She should have changed out of her shorts, but she was so busy being a superhero that she didn't think of it.

Her eyes danced from the windows to the front door as she crossed the yard, but she saw no movement in any of them by the time she got to the front steps. Of course, it was getting kind of dark.

Her footsteps on the pallets were pretty much the loudest thing she'd ever heard in her young life, and she wondered how Wyatt managed to sneak up on bad guys. At home, she knew where Wyatt was at all times. He wasn't exactly a bull in a china shop, but he was just so big. Too big to be sneaky. He'd been on all kinds of raids and busts; how did he not get shot every single day?

She instantly thought of Dwight and felt bad for thinking that, but in her family, fighting fear with humor was genetic.

Then, as she stood there trying to decide what to do, she heard the floor creaking just inside the door. She looked up at the door and waited a moment.

"Ryan?" she asked finally, her voice quieter than she'd expected. "Ryan, it's Sky Seward."

She waited for a moment, and was about to turn and run when she heard him, right up against the door.

"What are you doing here, Sky?" He sounded like an old man.

"I want to talk to you," she said. "Can you let me in?"

"That would be so stupid. Your mom is a cop."

"I know. But she's not here," Sky said. "Dude, I promise you nobody else knows where you are. I just—I just want you to let me try to help."

It took a moment for him to respond. Inside, the floor creaked as he shifted his weight.

"How did you know where I was?" he asked. He sounded more exhausted than suspicious, but the suspicion was there.

"I've been here before," she answered. "I recognized it."

"Great."

A moment later, he opened the door, slowly.

Sky had seen him in the video just a few minutes ago. Thirty, maybe. She'd seen then how worn out he looked, but in person, it was seriously startling. His pretty hair was starting to turn greasy, he had huge bags under his eyes, he was pale, and she could smell the stale sweat from his body. She hadn't been physically close to him in a long time, but she remembered that he always smelled like soap.

His t-shirt had dark stains in the armpits, and there were dark stains in the knees of his pants, too, like he'd been kneeling in the dirt for four days.

He looked over her shoulder, his eyes scanning the yard and road, and back to her. Then he seemed embarrassed, and looked down at the floor as he stepped back to let her in.

It took Sky's eyes a minute to adjust to the dim interior, even though it was twilight outside. The front door opened right into the room that was living room, dining room, and kitchen all in one, and it was pretty much the same as she remembered it.

The living room floor was covered with trash, old sofa cushions that Sky was positive should be cleansed with fire, and odd bits of a household, like a broken CD rack and the bottom of a lamp. The wall just in front of the door, the back wall of the living room, was covered in even more graffiti, and there was a washing machine with no door sitting up against a back window.

The kitchen counter was there, sort of like a breakfast bar, but all the appliances were gone and most of the cabinets were missing their doors. It was a cheerful place, the kind of place you wanted to be when you were depressed and scared out of your mind.

"Where's Adrian?" she asked after Ryan shut the door.

He lifted his right arm to point toward the kitchen, and that was the first time she realized he was holding the gun. He saw her see it and gave a small shrug.

"Sorry."

"You could put it down," she tried.

"The safety's on, if that helps."

"A little."

He walked toward the kitchen counter and she followed, praying that nothing disgusting touched her. He stopped at the end of the counter and she stopped, too. She remained several feet away, standing in the middle of the mauve shag carpet, the beer bottles and the used condoms.

He looked down at the floor, at something behind the counter. "Get up," he said quietly.

Sky heard the rustling of cloth against wood, and a moment later Adrian stood. He didn't look as bad as Ryan, but he didn't look a whole lot better, either. She didn't feel sorry for him, though. That was the difference. Although, she noticed that his permanent look of arrogance apparently wasn't all that permanent. He just looked hot and tired.

"I know you," he said. "You're in fourth-period lunch. Skyler. Yeah."

Sky didn't answer. She looked at Ryan. "Ryan, you have to make this stop," she said quietly.

He looked at her, and she couldn't remember seeing anybody look that sad. "How do I do that?" he asked.

"You're probably not in as much trouble as you think you are," Sky said.

He rubbed at his elbow with the gun. "You know, I've actually been worried that he was dead and they're keeping it a secret so they can get me to turn myself in to the police."

"He's not," Sky said. "Dwight's like family. I know. He's still in the ICU, but he made it through surgery."

Ryan looked at her with something sort of like gratitude, then he wobbled the gun in Adrian's direction. "Go back by the corner." He backed away a bit, making sure there was plenty of room between them.

Adrian sighed, then came around the counter and ambled past them. He looked at Sky as he went by. "You need to get your boyfriend to let me the hell out of here," he said. "I'm dying in here."

"Shut up, creep," she said forcefully. "If you can't pay the tab don't order the beer."

He glared at her, then slid down the wall and sat down. "You saying it's my fault I'm having a heatstroke in here? Cause I'm not the one that's got a gun."

"No, I'm not saying it's your fault," Sky replied. "Ryan's the one that picked up the gun, yeah. And he's gonna have to live with it. What I'm saying is that you watch enough YouTube that you should have seen it coming, dumbass." She swiped at her forehead with the back of her hand. "A really great guy, a truly good person, is in the hospital. I hope you've been having fun all year."

"Hey, I don't have to listen to you," Adrian said, jerking his chin up.

"Then don't," Sky said. "You won't understand half of what I say, anyway."

She looked over at Ryan, who had leaned back against the wall. He was staring at the floor, but his eyes were unfocused. His thoughts were somewhere else.

"Ryan."

He looked up at her.

"I know the cops that are looking for you," she said. "They're good people. Come with me. I mean, just get in my truck and come with me."

He shook his head slowly. "I shot a cop." His expression was almost one of amazement, if he was that animated. "I've never even been in a fight, and I shot a police officer."

"I know, but—"

He scratched at the corner of his eye. "Besides, I still kidnapped Adrian. That's what it is, you know."

"You can tell me about that later," Sky said. "We just need to make this stop. You need to let us help you—"

"I'm so tired," he interrupted. He tried to smile, but it wasn't a happy smile. "The only thing I could find in here to tie him up with was some old rope from a crab trap or something, and it broke in half when I tried to tie a stupid knot."

He sighed and leaned his head back against the wall, but his eyes were on Adrian. "So I have to just sit here, awake, watching him sleep. For three days, I've just been watching him sleep."

"That's not my fault, man," Adrian said, but the bravado was gone. He just sounded tired, too.

"I can't think anymore," Ryan said.

"Hey, it hasn't been some picnic for me, either," Adrian said, the resentment creeping back into his voice. He looked at Sky. "All night last night, he's over there talking to himself, trying to decide if he should blow his brains out, or let me go, or blow both our heads off."

Sky looked at Ryan. "Please don't do anything of those things, Ryan."

"What is it you think I should do, Sky?" He used his free hand to swipe at the sweat on his neck.

"Hey," Adrian said quietly. "Do you have any water or anything?" Sky looked over at him. "We already drank the water he had."

Sky looked at Ryan. "I have some Dr. Pepper in my truck. If I go get it, are you going to let me back in?"

He swallowed a couple of times, and she saw in his eyes how much he wanted it. She found that so horribly sad. A kid with a home and a mom that loved him, dying of thirst in the middle of a bunch of roach clips and used rubbers.

"You should just leave it on the steps and go home," Ryan said.

"Well, I gotta tell you, that would be pretty awesome," she said. "I would really like to just go home. But I can't."

She didn't wait for him to answer. She turned around, walked back out the door, and through the yard to her truck bed. She and some friends had gone to the beach the weekend before, and she knew for a fact she had a couple of sodas in the cooler. She flipped the lid up, and two cans of Dr. Pepper, half a bottle of orange juice, and a Ziploc bag of string cheese sloshed around in the warm water. She grabbed the sodas and the cheese, looked around to see if anyone was on the road, and then headed back to the trailer.

This time, she saw the blinds in the front window move, and Ryan opened the door when she got to the top of the rickety steps.

"What is that?" he asked hungrily when he saw the plastic bag.

"String cheese. Everything's hot, but it's still good."

She handed him one of the cans, and the bag of cheese, then held up the other can. "Can I give this to him?"

"Yeah."

Ryan popped the top of his can and started drinking. Sky walked over to Adrian and held out the other one. He looked a lot younger, looking up at her from the floor, and she almost felt sorry for him.

He took it without saying anything, popped it open, and took several long swallows. When he lowered the can to take a breath, Ryan threw two strips of cheese into his lap. He kept one for himself.

He sat back down against the wall, and after debating with himself for a minute, he hung onto the gun and tried to open the cheese with his teeth. Sky walked over and held out her hand.

"Give it to me."

He did, and she peeled the plastic off and handed it to him. Then she tossed the plastic on the floor.

"So you never answered me," Ryan said. "What do you think I should do?"

He didn't really sound like he cared about the answer, but she gave him one, anyway.

"I think you should come with me, and I'll take you to my mom."

"You got guts, I'll give you that," Adrian mumbled around his cheese.

Sky ignored him. "Ryan, I'm not gonna say that you turn yourself in and everything's fine, but your life isn't over, either. You can come back from it, eventually. He's not dead. They know it was an accident, too."

"Don't forget the kidnapping."

"Look, I'm just saying that you might not have the same life, but you will have a life to come back to."

"I don't have anything to come back to, Sky," Ryan said. "Even if I get out of prison eventually, then what? I have no scholarship, no college. I'm never going to be a vet. I've shamed my mom."

"I have a mother, too, you know," Adrian said.

Ryan looked over at Adrian, then back at Sky. "I didn't even get to finish what I was trying to say to her, because this guy has to be in the middle of everything."

Sky sighed. "So finish it."

He waved the gun a bit, as though to wave away her idea. She wasn't feeling it.

"Look, you don't know what you want to do, you don't know if you want to let him go, turn yourself in, run away…" She didn't include anything about blowing anybody's brains out. "At least say what you need to say to your mom. I saw her on TV. She seems like a nice lady."

"She is. She works really hard."

Sky reached back and slipped her phone out of her pocket. "Here, I'll film it—"

Ryan jumped up, the fastest she'd seen him move since she got there. "Oh, crap! Your phone! I didn't even—"

"What?"

"So they can track you, Sky?"

"Dude, chill out," she said quietly. She handed the phone to him. "I turned it off before I even left my house." He stared at it. "Take it. We'll use yours."

He looked up at her.

"You did it earlier. No cops are here," she said.

"That's because it was short."

"How short does it have to be?" she asked.

"I don't know." He almost laughed. "On TV, thirty seconds."

"Look, I don't know," Sky said, trying to look like she didn't think it was all that important. "If you don't want to, don't. You just mentioned it, that's all. I just want you to not feel like you're feeling right now."

Ryan swayed a little bit as he stood there, thinking about it. If Sky didn't know better, she would think he was just a little drunk.

"Okay, but short," he said.

"Okay, give me your phone."

He reached into his back pocket, turned it on, then opened his Facebook.

"Hurry, you're going to use up a lot of your time just getting there."

"Okay, here." He handed her the phone.

She held it up and pointed it at him, then sighed. "It's too dark, your face isn't even showing up." She looked around. "Hey, move."

"Me?" Adrian asked, like they'd woken him up.

"Well, yeah. Let him get over there where it's lighter," she said. "Come on, I need to turn this phone back off, dude."

"Okay, whatever."

Ryan watched Adrian walk to the middle of the room. "Over there by the counter," he said, pointing the gun in that direction.

He waited until Adrian was leaning on the counter, then he stood up against the wall where the other boy had just been. Sky looked at Adrian before she moved away from him a bit and turned her back to him.

"I can see you, and I'm pretty sure I can hit you from here, so don't go near her," Ryan said.

"All right, man. I don't care."

Sky held the phone up. "Okay, think about what you want to say, because we have to be really fast, ok?"

Ryan nodded and cleared his throat.

CHAPTER

EIGHTEEN

M aggie turned from Ellis Van Vleet onto 24th Avenue. She had been driving in a grid, but focusing on streets where she knew there were some empty buildings, especially houses.

Coco sat up-right in the back, looking out the window like she knew what they were looking for.

She waited for a white Escort to pull into its drive-way, then started moving south. A lot of the lots on 24th were deep, with a great deal of mature trees, and she tried to focus on going slowly enough to see beyond all the vegetation.

She'd gone two blocks when her phone buzzed on the passenger seat. She glanced over to see that it was Wyatt. She reached over and tapped at her phone to connect, unable to help remembering all the warnings she'd given the kids about texting while driving.

"Hey," she said on speaker.

"Hey, he's on Facebook live. Right now," Wyatt said. "Where are you?"

"Crap! On 24th. Let me find a place to pull over," she said.

She drove another hundred feet, checked her rear-view, and then yanked the Jeep over onto the swale. She heard Coco's nails scrape against the leather, heard her tags jingle as she slid sideways in the seat. She glanced over her shoulder to make sure Coco was okay, then she slammed the Jeep into park and picked up the phone. She took herself off speaker. "Okay, what's he saying? Is Sky there?"

"Slow down. It's over," Wyatt said, "But Myles record-ed it. We won't have the comments, but we'll have the video. But she's not in it, Maggie."

"Did you watch it?"

"No, I'm on my way over to the airport. I'm gonna start looking over there. I'll take the east side, and Quin-cy's starting on the west. We still don't know if she's in that tower's range. We're working on pinging his phone, but—"

"I want to see it," she said.

"I know, just hold on."

He put her on hold and had just come back on the line when her phone buzzed.

"He just sent you a link to Google or Drive or some crap," Wyatt said, the tension in his voice getting thicker.

"Go ahead and look at it. I'm coming off the bridge into town."

"Okay."

Maggie disconnected him, then clicked on the text message. It took her to Dropbox. She clicked on the video, and there was Ryan again. He was farther away from the camera this time, at least six or eight feet. Someone was holding that phone.

"Mom, I just have a minute," Ryan said. If possible, he looked worse than he had the last time. "I just wanted to tell you that I'm really sorry about—"

Maggie hit stop and stared at the wall behind him, at the graffiti scrawled all over it.

At the graffiti that was just above and to the right of his head.

She thumbed back to her home screen, tapped her phone open, and called Wyatt back.

"Yeah."

"Wyatt, I know where she is!"

"Where?"

"She's in that old trailer on Oyster Road!"

"Oyster Road," he mumbled. "Where the hell is that?"

"Right off of Brownsville," she said. "It's the next left after you pass West Pine."

"How do you know she's there?" In the background, Maggie heard someone honking.

"The graffiti. That wall you saw, he's in front of it," she said. "It says *Bella was here*, in big blue letters."

"Sky's Bella?"

"Yes! Do you remember about three or four years ago, when I busted Sky and Bella? They were supposed to be staying at Bella's and her Mom didn't know anything about it when I called. We finally got one of their other friends to cop that they went with some older kids to this place on Oyster Road."

"Hold on," Wyatt said. "Okay, what's the address?"

"I don't know. You'll have to look on Google Maps. If you take Brownsville west, the first left after West Pine is Oyster. It's just a bunch of scrubby woods, but the next curve, like a block down, there's a beat to hell trailer. That's where it is."

"I'm calling it in. Wait for me. I'm five minutes away."

"No. I'll call you when I get there."

"Maggie."

"I'm not going in, Wyatt, but I'm going. There's good visibility of the road from the trailer, so everybody needs to either pull into the back of the lot across the road or come from the other way and park in those woods."

She checked her side mirror, then glanced in the rearview at Coco. "Hold on, baby." Coco sat down.

Maggie checked the traffic again, then pulled back onto 24th. She was two minutes away. There was no point in using the siren. Ryan would hear it as well as anybody.

"Maggie."

"I'll see you in a few minutes." She just caught his 'dammitall' before she disconnected.

She went faster than she wanted to know about all the way down Brownsville, slowing only when she came to the intersection with West Pine. This end of Brownsville was primarily undeveloped, save for a few businesses, and storage parks. She was the only one on the road until she turned off it.

The trailer was located about a block down, right in the curve where the road eased to the left. Her best place to go was the undeveloped land on the right side of Oyster; the south side of that abutted the lot the trailer was on. Somebody might still spot her from the trailer, but only if they happened to be looking in the five seconds it took her to approach the empty lot and then pull into the trees.

She barely glanced to her left as she pulled in, but she registered Sky's truck out front. For just a moment, she got that sensation in her stomach that she had when she was about to fall asleep, that odd moment of being without gravity as she dreamed that she was falling.

That feeling was gone by the time she turned off the Cherokee. It was replaced by the steady warmth of immediacy, the almost calming adrenaline of being on a scene at a critical time. She got it when she was in on busts, she got it when she was about to draw her weapon. It was the odd combination of fear of the unknown and the focus of training and experience. It was a lot better than a mother's stark terror.

Coco whined softly in the back, and Maggie wondered if she had seen the truck, too.

Her position didn't give her much of a view of the trailer's lot, and even less a view of the trailer itself. She looked over her shoulder at Coco, who was standing, ready to jump out of the car and help, whatever Maggie was trying to do.

"Stay here, baby," Maggie said quietly, then she grabbed her phone, opened her door and got out.

She moved deeper into the lot, around trees and through bushes, until she was directly across from and beside the trailer. Now she could see Adrian Nichols' car parked in the back, parallel to the mobile home. Just a few yards beyond it was more woods.

She tapped her phone and called Wyatt back.

"I'm turning onto Brownsville," he said by way of hello. "Where are you?"

"The lot at the corner. Adrian's car is in back and Sky's truck is in front."

"See anybody?"

"No, but that doesn't mean they didn't see me."

"We've got units from PD that are coming in from the south side," Wyatt said. "Quincy and some of the other guys are going to approach from the other side. Where you are, I guess."

"Yeah." Maggie moved back the way she'd come until she could see the front of the trailer again. Still no movement. The sight of Sky's Toyota made an instant sheen of sweat develop above her upper lip.

"We're not hiding," Wyatt said. "Going in no sirens, nice and calm, but with numbers. Let's see if we can get this kid to talk."

"Yeah."

"I'm pulling in," Wyatt said. A moment later, the crunch of gravel sounded behind her and she turned to watch him park next to the Cherokee.

She walked toward him as he got out.

⚓   ⚓   ⚓

Ten minutes later, units were in place on either side of the trailer, with cruisers blocking Oyster at both ends. Quincy and several other deputies had joined Maggie and Wyatt in the undeveloped lot. They'd been discussing the best way to approach Ryan Warner, who undoubtedly knew they were there, unless he was unable to know it, which was something no one voiced.

Everyone had donned their body armor and attached their radios to their shoulders. No one wanted anything other than a peaceful surrender brought about by convincing communication, but everyone prepared for something far less ideal.

"We checked," Quincy was saying. "His phone's still off."

Wyatt held up a finger and touched his earpiece.

"Okay," Wyatt said. "Lon Woodman is reporting that someone was messing with the blinds in front," he said. "So…we have movement inside."

Everyone knew what he meant. Someone was alive inside. The concern, among many, was the tone of the video that had led them here. The opinion was pretty unanimous that it sounded a lot like a suicide note. The kid was exhausted and under a great deal of duress. Not the kind of conditions that encouraged reasonable thought.

Maggie stared at the ground as Wyatt went on, not wanting anyone to have to look her in the eye.

R yan yanked his fingers out of the blinds and spun to glare wildly at Sky.

"How could you *do* this?"

"I'm trying to help," Sky said, her voice cracking against her will.

"Help? Why didn't you just stay home, stay out of it?" he yelled. "Nobody wants to just leave me alone!"

"They can't, Ryan," she said. "They can't."

"It's all his fault!"

He swung his gun arm to point at Adrian, still standing at the counter. Sky didn't know if he even realized he was pointing with the gun, but it made her heart pound even faster, and Adrian had gone pale.

"I'm sorry, man!" he said. "I said I was sorry!"

"I don't care! I'm sorry, too!" Ryan stepped from one foot to the other, weaving like a caged cat. "You think *I'm* not sorry? I've lost everything! Everything!"

"Ryan, not everything. You can still have a life one day." It sounded weak and stupid, even to her.

"Really?" he asked, leaning toward her. "Really? I shot a police officer."

"It was an accident," she said.

"It doesn't matter, Sky! I wasn't supposed to have the gun! Not to mention kidnapping," he said, sweeping the gun in Adrian's direction. "I've seen enough *Law & Order*, Sky. That's a federal offense. You basically go to prison forever for that."

"What were you even thinking, dude?" she asked gently.

"I don't know! I was just angry! I don't remember what I was thinking," he answered. "It was his fault and I just wanted to scare him the way he scared me!"

"Well, I'm scared," Adrian said, his voice so quiet Sky almost didn't hear him.

"I want you to get out," Ryan said, and his tone had gone from frantic to determined. "I want you to just go, Sky. Get out of here."

"Why?"

He leaned in close.

"Because I don't want you here!" he yelled.

"No."

"Geez, you're stupid," Adrian said.

Ryan spun around to face him. "Shut up!" Adrian stepped back until he was right up against the counter.

"Ryan, let me call my mom," Sky said, trying to find a calming tone.

"What for? She's already here, right? She's got to be out there with all of them!"

"Because we can tell her how it is," Sky said. "We can let them see that you're not dangerous." She didn't know if that was actually true; he just wasn't in a frame of mind that she could predict. She believed in her heart that he never meant to hurt anyone, but now she was pretty sure he could hurt himself, or Adrian, or all three of them. She felt he was most likely to hurt himself.

"They don't care, Sky! It's not their job to care!"

"She cares."

His eyes were wild when he looked at her then. Wide with desperation.

"She cares about you, and she cares about her friend," he said.

"Ryan, if you don't talk to them somehow, if you don't start talking to them, they're going to come in here. Listen to me, let me call her and ask her to come in and talk to you. She will, and no one is going to do anything with her in here."

He looked over at Adrian, then looked up at the ceiling and sighed. He stood there for a moment, his body swaying just enough to notice, and Sky actually thought about trying to take him while the gun was pointed at the floor.

It was a stupid thought, and fleeting. Yeah, her mom had taught her to defend herself. Wyatt had taught her how to snap the neck of any boy who asked her out on a date, but she wasn't some TV cop. Standing here, one foot away from someone who had a gun in his hand and who wasn't thinking clearly, it was scary, and her feet were rooted.

She wanted her mother. She wanted Wyatt. She wanted to go home, but she did not want Ryan to get hurt. She didn't want him to hurt *himself*, and she didn't even know why she cared so much.

"I don't know what to do," he said to himself. "I don't know how to make this stop."

"Ryan," she said calmly. Slowly. "If you don't talk to my mom, that's not going to be your decision."

⚓ ⚓ ⚓

Quincy listened to the voice in his earpiece. "Roger that." He looked up at the rest of them, who were waiting. "SWAT's still at least twenty minutes out," he said.

SWAT was part of the Franklin County Sheriff's Office, and would ordinarily have been on scene in a probable hostage situation. Unfortunately, SWAT was on a meth bust way out in Tate's Hell.

"I don't think we should wait for SWAT," Maggie said.

"I can swing either way," Wyatt said, his face grim. "But let's see if we can try to get somewhere here in the meantime. Let's get the horn and try to communicate with him."

Maggie's phone vibrated, and when she pulled it out her pulse sped up. "It's Ryan." She didn't wait for someone to tell her what to say or do. She answered.

"Hello," she said.

"Mom."

Maggie took a breath, let it out slowly. "Sky."

"Mom, Ryan says he'll let you come in and talk to him, but just you."

"Okay. Am I on speaker?"

"Yeah."

She opened her mouth, and Wyatt shoved a finger up in the air to stop her from speaking.

"Okay. Ryan, I can come in there and talk with you," she said anyway, and in the corner of her eye, she saw Wyatt turn his back to her, hands on his hips. "But can you let Sky and Adrian out first?"

"I told Sky to leave," she heard him say from nearby.

"Sky, come on out here, and let me come in and talk to Ryan."

"I can't."

"Why?"

"I can't, Mom."

"I'm not keeping her here!" Ryan said over her, raising his voice. He sounded like he was deteriorating.

"He doesn't want to hurt anybody, Mom."

"Then we need to talk about this calmly and rationally and find a way for all of us to be safe."

"She can come in, but that's it. Nobody else," she heard Ryan say.

"That's fine, Ryan," Maggie said quietly. Wyatt turned around and mouthed for her to put him on hold. She looked down at the ground. "Ryan, I want to help you. I promise you, that's what we all want."

"She can come in, but no gun," she heard him insist.

"He says no gun," Sky said.

"I heard him."

"And if she's got one of those vests like those guys are wearing, I want her to take it off!"

There was a fumbling sound over the phone, like Sky had put a hand over it or held it away.

"Dude, my mom's not coming in here without a vest," she said, almost whispering.

"She will if she wants to come in here," Ryan said. He sounded like he was across the room. He was moving.

"I can do that," Maggie said.

"No, I'm telling you that my mom is *not* coming in here without a vest," Sky was saying over her. "You're scared and you haven't slept and you have a gun. We don't need another accidental cop shooting!"

"No vest," Ryan said back, more quietly.

"Forget it, Mom," Sky said it into the phone.

"No vest, Ryan," Maggie said loudly. "Five minutes."

She disconnected the call before realizing she was disconnecting her daughter, not just the boy with the gun. She could hear the echo of Sky's voice in her ear, and now her little girl suddenly seemed far away.

She lowered her phone and looked at Wyatt. He pressed his lips together, not looking at her, and she knew how angry he really was. She put the phone in her back pocket and started removing her body armor.

"Maggie, I don't think this is such a hot idea," Quincy said, shaking his head. "Come on."

"I know it's not, Quince," she said quietly, ripping open the Velcro at her waist.

"Boss?" Quincy asked Wyatt.

Wyatt looked up and glared at Maggie. He crooked his finger. "Come with me."

She followed him over to Quincy's cruiser, about ten feet away, as she opened the other side of her vest. Wyatt stopped and turned on her.

"We won't get into how pissed I am."

"I know you're pissed." She took off the vest.

"We won't get into how pissed I am," he said again. She craned her neck to look up at him. "Do you have your back-up weapon on you?"

"Yes."

"Give it to me."

"Why?"

"Because he watches TV."

She bent down and removed the little .380 from her ankle holster. He took it from her, jerked her around by the shoulder, and shoved it into the back of her waistband.

"Show him the holster, but keep your back to him if you can," he said tersely.

"He'll probably ask me to turn around, anyway," she said. "Then he'll be just as pissed."

"Maybe," he said, jerking her back around. "But you've got a better shot of drawing it from your waist than you do from your ankle."

"I don't want to shoot this kid."

"Nobody wants to shoot this kid," he said. He put his hands on his hips, then keyed his shoulder mic. "Mike, you and Lon take positions at the back door, Steve and Porter be ready to move around the front. Maggie's going inside. Move into position once she's in."

He let go of the mic and looked at her. "Get him to let her out—"

"He *told* her to get out—"

"Then make her go!" he snapped. "Then I know you'll be thinking more about how you're getting out."

"It's going to be okay," she said, though she had no way of knowing if that was true.

"You don't know *what* it's going to be," he said. "That kid is in a volatile and possibly suicidal state of mind. Get Sky out of there, get Adrian out if he's still breathing, and then if he wants to blow his head off, you let him. Don't rush him because you think you can save him."

"Wyatt, I am going to go in there and do the best that I can to keep everybody safe," she said. "I'm going to try to talk to this kid and get everybody out of that dump alive. And then I am going to go home and beat the hell out of my daughter."

"Our daughter," he snapped, but she heard the hurt there. They might have only been married for a few months, but Wyatt had known Sky since she was seven.

"Yes," she said. "Our daughter, and we will beat her together."

He looked into her eyes and sighed. "Bledsoe and the FDLE and the Sheriff's Office are all right, you know. The policy is right. We can't work together like this anymore."

"We've done just fine in the past."

"Not anymore," he said. "They're right. It impairs judgment. I do need to stick to talking to the press and speaking at the Neighborhood Watch luncheons."

"Well, you can do that later," she said. She thumbed open her phone, tapped her contacts, and clicked to dial Wyatt. She put it on speaker, and he frowned at her as his phone vibrated in his back pocket. He pulled it out as she dropped hers into her shirt pocket.

"I'll keep it open," she said, as he connected the call. She turned around. "I love you."

"I love you, too," he said quietly as he followed her back to the group. "But wait till I get you home."

$$ ⚓ \quad ⚓ \quad ⚓ $$

Ryan peered through the space in the blinds. A woman with long, dark hair like Sky's, tied up in a ponytail, was walking across the yard. She was wearing blue cargo pants and a t-shirt, and she had her hands up in the air.

Behind her, on the street, the other cops were still watching from behind their cruisers. They had their guns drawn and resting against the hoods and roofs. All pointed at him. He knew there were more cops over in the woods, where she'd come from.

There were so many cops. So many, and he didn't know how he had gotten here.

He looked over his shoulder at Sky. "Your mom is coming in."

Sky swallowed hard but didn't say anything. Adrian was still over by the counter, staring at the front door.

Ryan looked back out the window, as the woman stopped about two feet in front of the steps.

"Ryan?" she called. "I'm here. Can you let me in?"

He pulled his fingers from the blinds and stood.

"Wait," Sky said. "Stay away from the door."

She started for the door, waving him back from the window. "Go over there. I'll let her in."

CHAPTER

TWENTY

Maggie carefully climbed the clumsily construct-
ed steps, the old wooden pallets groaning underneath her weight. She stopped at the top step.

"Ryan? It's Maggie."

She heard the floor creak inside, and then the door
opened halfway. Sky stood there, eyes wide, face pale.
She looked like she might cry, and Maggie was overwhelmed by an onslaught of different feelings; relief,
fear, anger, all swirling together like the conflicting and
countering of confused seas.

"Are you okay, Sky?" she asked, her calm voice surprising even to her.

"Yeah, Mom," Sky said. "I'm sorry."

"Can I come in?"

Sky hesitated.

"Let her in," Ryan said from somewhere behind Sky.
It was almost dark outside and even darker in the old
trailer.

Sky stepped back without opening the door any wider, and Maggie edged in, keeping her hands in the air. She looked around quickly, as Sky closed the door.

The place was even filthier than she remembered. Old furniture, couch cushions, blankets. Every conceivable soda or beer bottle. She was glad she was wearing boots.

She saw Ryan first, standing over near the back wall. His arm was bent, the gun resting on his chest. It was too dark to see for sure, but she knew his hands were shaking. He was clearly terrified. Terrified and something else. Defeated, she finally decided. Defeated could be good or bad. He might be weary enough to surrender, or hopeless enough to turn the gun on himself, and possibly everyone else beforehand.

After a few seconds, she saw Adrian Nichols standing in front of the kitchen counter. His hair hung damply around his pale face, and he looked as terrified as he should be. Maggie looked back at Sky, who was standing beside her.

"Move over there," she said quietly, jerking her head toward the kitchen.

Sky looked like she was going to ask why, but she glanced over at Ryan, and then crossed the few yards over to the where Adrian was standing. She kept as much distance between her and the other boy as she could. Ryan's eyes bounced between Sky and Maggie, then settled nervously on Maggie.

"Hello, Ryan," she said quietly.

"Sky looks just like you," he said.

"She's like me in a lot of ways," Maggie said.

"Why is your phone lit up?"

"My team is listening in," she answered. "They have to. That's the only way they'd let me come in."

"So they can come in here with guns blazing?" He sounded more exhausted than confrontational.

"Yes," Maggie said. "If they hear people being hurt, or about to be hurt, that is what they'll probably do."

"I never meant to hurt anybody."

"Nobody out there wants to hurt anybody, either."

"It was an accident," Ryan said, wiping his neck. "I panicked."

"So it seems," Maggie answered. "I want to talk to you about that, but I'm going to be honest with you. The SWAT team will be here in about ten minutes, and they have authority over the scene in a hostage situation."

"I didn't—" He rubbed his left eye with the back of his gun hand. "Hostages. Damn," he added quietly, maybe to himself.

"Ryan, they'll be a lot more likely to let us decide how to end this situation if you let Sky and Adrian go outside. I'll stay here with you."

"Mom—"

Maggie looked at her. "You made your call," she said evenly. "Now you stay out of it."

"She was trying to help me," Ryan said.

"I know that," she answered, nodding. "You need to let her go, okay? They won't come in here for me, but they will for her, or for Adrian. That's just the way it is. Procedure."

Ryan leaned back against the wall. He looked like he hadn't slept since he'd gotten up to go to school Thursday.

"I told her to go before," he said.

"I know. They know outside, too. Can I put my hands down?"

He stared at her for a moment. "Yeah."

She lowered her hands. "I want to show you something, okay?" She tugged at the knee of her pants, exposing her empty ankle holster, then let it go. "I'm not here to hurt you. I promise you that's not what I want."

He didn't answer, and she went on.

"I need you to let Sky and Adrian go outside."

"I told her to go. I don't want her here," he said.

"What about Adrian?"

"I don't want him here, either!" he said, his voice rising. "I don't want anybody here!"

"Okay," she said calmly. "I understand. But I can't help being here. I can't leave."

"I just want to be left alone," he said, and he sounded a hundred years old.

Maggie looked over at Sky. "Go. You and Adrian go outside."

Sky looked over at Ryan, but he was staring into space.

"I want to stay with you," she said, almost whispering.

"Go!" Ryan yelled, making her jump. "Get out!"

Adrian started for the door, passing Sky. After another look at Ryan, Sky followed.

Maggie watched Ryan watch them cross the room. Keeping her back to the door, she moved out of the way a bit so they could pass. Sky was staring at her, and Maggie nodded at her. Then she heard the door open, heard Adrian, far heavier than Sky, as he ran down the steps. Then the door closed quietly, and she heard her daughter's much softer, much slower steps follow.

⚓   ⚓   ⚓

None of the cops in the street moved a muscle, but as soon as Sky and Adrian hit the woods of the empty lot, Quincy and another deputy sprinted over to lead them deeper in. Wyatt almost ran them over as he grabbed Sky's arm and pulled her to him. He kissed her hard on the forehead as he heard Maggie's voice through the phone, sounding too far away.

"Okay, Ryan," she said. "They're safe. Now how do I help you get safe, too?"

TWENTY-ONE

Ryan looked across the room at her, his face almost lost to the shadow. "Why can't you just leave? Please?"

Maggie swallowed. "I can't do that, Ryan. I'm supposed to be here."

"Well, I'm not," he said. "I'm supposed to be some-place else."

"What do you mean?" she asked, taking a few steps closer.

"I should be at the beach, or at home, somewhere."

"Yes, you should. And I'm sorry that you aren't," she said. "But we need to get you out of here. Safely."

He glared at her. "You can't tell me that it's all going to be okay because it isn't! Nothing is okay!"

"No, nothing is." She kept moving toward him, not trying to hide it, but slowly. "But it doesn't have to be as bad as it is right now."

"You think I don't know how much trouble I'm in? I ruined everything!" He thumped the side of the gun against his forehead. "Stupid! Stupid! A gun!"

"Ryan!" He looked at her and took a shaky breath. "Can you tell me why you took the gun to school?"

"I don't *know* why!" She saw the glint of tears in his eye. "I saw the video when I was getting ready for school, and I got so angry! I was…humiliated and angry! And I snuck into my mom's room and I got the gun."

He looked at her, and the anguish in his face was plain.

"By the time I got on the bus, I was like, what are you doing, Ryan, are you nuts? But I was already on the bus, and then I was at school, and I couldn't just throw it somewhere."

"Okay. I get that," she said.

"But then they got off the bus and I could see they were waiting for me, and I was scared. And mad. I didn't want to get off the bus, but the driver was telling me to hurry up because the little kids were waiting to get off. And I got off."

He wiped his sleeve against his forehead with his gun arm, then rested the gun against his chest again.

"I got off and they started hassling me right away," he went on. "And I was scared and I was so angry, and I just wanted them to be scared, too. I wanted them to know what it felt like! And I pulled out the gun without even thinking about it. It was like it wasn't even me in here," he said, thumping his chest with the gun.

"And Deputy Shultz was there."

"Yeah." His mouth twisted, then she saw a tear run down his cheek, cleaning a tiny path through the dirt and dust and sweat. He blinked, trying to clear the tears away. "He was trying to help."

"I know."

"I keep seeing his face," he said. "When the gun went off. It was like he just couldn't believe it. Like he couldn't believe that had happened to him."

Maggie swallowed. She could see it. Had seen it. No, Dwight couldn't believe it.

"He's going to be okay," she said gently, and hoped it was true.

Ryan looked her in the eye, and she saw desperation give way to hopelessness. "Nothing is going to be okay."

His hand shifted, and the gun tilted upward, until the barrel was under his chin.

"Ryan," Maggie said carefully. "Please."

He started crying, his eyes squeezed shut. She couldn't just take the gun from him. The safety was off, and she would most likely just help him blow a hole through his skull.

"Everybody, please," she said. "Everybody just please stay put. Ryan, look at me. Please."

He opened his eyes. "No, I ruined everything. My whole life." He gasped, a fresh slew of tears falling. "My mom's life. I've ruined her life, too. She's such a good person. I can't—I ruined everything!"

Maggie's breath hitched as she saw his hand tighten on the gun, saw him squeeze his eyes shut and wince.

"Ryan, please don't do this to her!" she said quickly. He opened his eyes, but just barely. She doubted he could see her well, anyway, in the dark and through his tears.

"Ryan, I'm a mom," she said more quietly. "I can survive anything...*anything*, except the loss of my child. I don't care how bad it is, how much trouble, how awful it is. I can survive anything, except losing one of them."

She held her hand out, palm up. His eyes didn't leave hers.

"Please, baby."

⚓ ⚓ ⚓

Maggie saw Wyatt come to the edge of the yard as she walked Ryan toward the wooded lot. She kept one hand under Ryan's elbow and held his weapon and magazine in the other. She saw Sky appear next to Wyatt, and saw Wyatt gently reach over and push her back.

The officers who had been at the ready behind their cruisers had holstered their weapons and stood. Lon and Mike had come out from the positions at the side of the trailer and were walking on the other side of Ryan.

They got to the edge of the lot, and Maggie met Wyatt's eye. He didn't say anything to her; he just let out a slow breath, then looked down at Ryan. "Ryan, I need you to go with Deputy Quincy here."

Quincy stepped up, and Maggie let go of Ryan. Quince took that arm, Lon took the other, and they led him over to Quincy's cruiser.

Wyatt looked back at Maggie, then started removing his vest as he walked toward one of the other cruisers, where Adrian Nichols sat in the back, legs hanging out the open door. He was drinking a bottle of water, and another deputy was talking to him.

Sky looked over her shoulder as they led Ryan away, then looked back at Maggie.

"I'm sorry, Mom."

Maggie had so much to say, and couldn't say it all at once. None of it went together anyway; the anger mixed with the fear, the understanding with the disbelief. She looked away, toward her Jeep, where she could hear Coco keening through the cracked windows.

"I really am sorry." Sky blinked back tears.

Maggie sighed, and then leaned over and buried her face in her daughter's neck.

She smelled of sweat and mint and gardenia body wash, and Maggie could finally breathe again.

⚓ ⚓ ⚓

Adrian held the bottle of water up to his face, rolled it around on his forehead, and couldn't believe how good it felt when the condensation started dripping down into his eyes.

He looked over at the cluster of cops, all of them standing around in a circle with their hands on their hips or resting on their holsters, talking in quiet voices. A few of the other cops were walking Ryan to one of the cop cars. Adrian expected him to look over at him, but he didn't.

He'd been sure, since the chick was a cop's daughter, that they were going to bust in there and shoot his ass. Or that the lady cop would, Sky's mom. He'd seen the gun in the back of her pants when he was getting out, and the whole rest of the time they were in there, he kept bracing to hear the pop.

As soon as he thought it, he felt a twinge of guilt. He didn't like Warner, never had. Disliked him on sight. He'd had fun giving him a hard time. He liked the feeling of power it gave him. He could trip the loser in the hallway and sleep just fine that night. He didn't even feel bad when he and Newman posted the video of him with piss on his pants.

But he had this sudden vision of how Warner had looked two weeks ago, or how he had looked the other day, and he couldn't help wondering if he had made the Ryan he saw in the biology lab look like the Ryan that had just come out of the trailer.

There was this small feeling in his chest, like some little animal scratching at him, that said that he had.

It was mostly Newman's fault; that fat-ass was always egging him on, but while Ryan and the cop had still been inside, while he'd been outside waiting for the shot to come, he'd had this feeling. This nervous feeling, that if they blew Ryan Warner away tonight, he was going to be dealing with it someway tomorrow.

CHAPTER
TWENTY-TWO

Maggie came out of the bathroom and into their bedroom, Coco trailing behind her. She fidgeted with the waistband of her dress, straightening it and smoothing it out. It was one of two good dresses she owned, but still not remotely fancy. Pale yellow, with tiny flowers of blue and white, it was more casual than a bridesmaid's dress but more formal than jeans. It was what she had.

She slid her feet into a pair of yellow sandals and looked over at Wyatt, who was standing in front of the dresser mirror. Stoopid was perched right in front of him, warbling away.

"Stoopid, if I wanted to tie a Windsor knot, I would have already done it," Wyatt said as he finished with his tie.

"Be careful," Maggie said, smiling. "You're getting to be as bad as me."

"No, I am not," Wyatt said. "I'm just humoring him."

He straightened his white dress shirt, tucking it more neatly into his gray trousers. Wyatt hated dressing up, too, preferring shorts and one of his Hawaiian shirts, but he still looked more appropriate than Maggie felt.

"You look nice," Maggie said.

"I know. I'm thinking I might hit on some of the other moms."

"Oh, I forgot you were a jerk," Maggie said.

"Sure you did." He stopped in front of her and put his hands on her waist. "You're just pretending you did to get back on my good side."

"Okay, yeah," Maggie said. "I mean, I've had to have sex with you, and everything."

"Especially everything," Wyatt countered.

Sky's voice popped up from the open doorway.

"Could we please at least make it to coffee without me having to barf all over the place?"

Sky looked so beautiful that Maggie wanted her to go change. To go put on something she would wear any other Saturday so that Maggie could have a little more time.

Her hair was up in its usual bun, though a little bit neater, and she'd been very careful with her modest but immaculate make-up. She was wearing a dress that she'd bought back in May. It was a black sheath that hugged her figure and hung to her knees and made her look like a twenty-five-year-old woman.

"You're going to miss our little conversations when you're gone, kiddo," Wyatt said.

"Oh, yeah," Sky said, rolling her eyes.

"Maybe we can Skype you when we're flirting, so you don't get homesick."

"OMG, you're helpless," she said. "Why would you Skype when you can just FaceTime me on your phone? But don't."

Maggie pulled away from Wyatt. "Can you go see if Kyle's ready?"

"You mean can I bug off? Sure."

He walked out of the room, kissing the top of Sky's head as he passed. Maggie walked over to her.

"You look incredible."

"Thanks."

Maggie sighed. "Are you excited?"

"Yeah, sure. I don't have to remember a locker combination anymore." Maggie smiled at her. "Of course I'm excited, but not because I'm abandoning my mother, so don't get all goopy and crazy, okay?"

"Okay."

Sky wrapped her arms around her mother's neck and sighed. "Geez, dude."

Maggie breathed in deeply. Gardenias.

⚓ ⚓ ⚓

Maggie and Wyatt sat in the second row of the parents' section. Kyle was a couple of rows back with Maggie's parents, who had gotten back a few days earlier. Maggie had seen Boudreaux too, but he had slipped away into the crowd.

The day was cloudy and overcast, but there was a nice breeze, and Maggie didn't have to fight the sun's glare on her phone. She had already stuck it up over the head of the blond man in front of her when Sky walked up to the podium.

It took her just a moment to start speaking, but her voice was clear and strong, her head high.

"I started writing my valedictorian speech weeks ago," she started. "I went through seven drafts of a speech about becoming leaders in our communities, and I hated every one of them. But a week ago, I wrote a new speech. Something that I could actually stand up here and say, and know that what I was saying was from my heart."

She glanced down at the podium for a moment before speaking again.

"We were born into a world that has never been seen before. A world where a high school student in Franklin County can build a lasting friendship with a high schooler in Kenya. A world where it seems like at least half of life is lived online. It's a world where the cure for cancer is right at our fingertips, and where we see, all the time, that one person really can make a difference, no matter what age they are."

She stopped, took a breath, and went on.

"The internet and social media have made it possible, just in our lifetimes, to make the world smaller, more accessible, and safer. To make us more tolerant, kinder, and more aware." Sky stopped and looked around the first few rows of students. "But the internet and social media have also created unprecedented opportunities for every one of us to fall short of our potential as human beings. Kids our age, and much younger, live for their fifteen minutes of internet fame and don't care how they get it. Life isn't lived, it's only photographed and shared. Friendships aren't built with experiences shared face to face but with a click and a Like."

Maggie saw the man in front of her, and his wife, shift a little in their seats.

"Kids like us, the ones born into this generation, have a much greater chance of being bullied and tormented and stalked, and kids like us have much greater opportunities to humiliate, frighten, and attack others."

"Good for you, kid," Wyatt said under his breath.

"This isn't the only reason that teen suicides have increased dramatically," Sky said. "It isn't the only reason that it's almost common for a kid to walk into a high school or public place and open fire. But I believe, in my heart, that it is one of the biggest reasons."

Sky glanced over towards Maggie.

"When my mom went to this high school just twenty years ago, school violence meant two kids fighting in the parking lot. Now it means a kid walking into the school and killing dozens."

Sky paused a moment and put her hands on either side of the podium. Maggie couldn't believe she looked so self-assured. The girl who, two years ago, couldn't speak without rolling her eyes.

"We were born into this new world, and in just a few minutes, we will be graduating into a world that we can change. *We* are the ones who can work to exploit the good possibilities of the internet without exploiting each other. *We* are the ones who can make it clear that it is never okay for a kid to take a gun to school, and *we* are the ones who can change the circumstances that make that kid think he or she wants to."

Sky paused and scanned the crowd of students in front of her, most of whom she had known her whole life.

"We are the generation who can turn bullies into outcasts and the bullied into victors. We are the generation who can make it cool to stand up for others and shameful to tear them down. We are the ones who can put the internet back into its rightful place, and start living in and experiencing the real world again. A world that is safer, more exciting, and more uplifting than it was when we woke up this morning."

She stopped, took a smooth breath, and let it out.

"We can't un-invent the internet or social media, but we can reinvent how we use them. We can't undo the tragedy and violence that have already taken place, but we can work to change the climate that allowed them." Sky looked up from her notes.

"We come from a very small part of Florida. We come from a very tiny part of the world, but that doesn't mean that we're too small to change it."

She looked out at the crowd and gave a smile. "Thank you."

The crowd burst into enthusiastic applause, and Maggie would have joined in, but she was still holding her phone high. She brought it down when the row of parents in front of her stood.

She stood, too, and turned the phone around. "Did you catch it all?" she asked, beaming.

Dwight's face was almost as pale as the hospital pillows, and the FaceTime app wasn't necessarily kind, but he looked good.

"Reckon I'm crying 'cause they took my Percocet away?" Dwight asked, smiling.

He shoved himself up a little bit further in the bed. "I'd stand and applaud but they still haven't brought me my underwear."

⚓   ⚓   ⚓

The 10th book in the Forgotten Coast Florida Suspense series, *Overboard*, will be out in August. Until then, have you started the spin-off Still Waters series, featuring Wyatt's good friend, Sheriff Evan Caldwell? If not, read on for a look at the first book in the series, *Dead Reckoning*.

⚓   ⚓   ⚓

THE END

The 10th book in the Forgotten
Coast Florida Suspense series,

OVERBOARD

will be out in August. Until then,
have you started the spin-off Still
Waters series, featuring Wyatt's
good friend, Sheriff Evan Caldwell?
If not, read on for a look at the first
book in the series,

DEAD RECKONING.

ONE

People who dream about quiet country nights have never been in the country after dark.

Even after their dogs had shut up, Mooney White and Grant Woodburn were surrounded by nothing but noise. The crickets and the frogs were screaming at each other, and there was a light breeze, nice for June, moving through the trees that had been bothersome to the men before they'd finally bagged their fill.

It was just past three in the morning, and dark-dark. The men were in the ass end of Gulf County, FL, in the woods just north of Wewahitchka and near the Dead Lakes Recreation Area. The low, thick cloud cover made the moon pointless.

Mooney was a black man in his late forties. He was dressed in an old pair of his blue work pants and a navy windbreaker. The many spots of white in his close-cropped hair looked like a little patch of fireflies in the night. He used his flashlight to guide their steps over rocks and fallen limbs. His .22 rifle was slung over his shoulder, and he held his dog's leash in the other hand.

Grant Woodburn, a redheaded man just a bit younger than his best friend, held his dog's leash in one hand, and a .410 single shot in the other. Their bag of coons was slung around his neck.

The men's boots crunched softly atop the thick carpet of pine needles. Ahead of them, the two dogs were almost soundless in their passage.

It was Mooney who first spotted the dim lights. They rounded a thick copse of shrubs and old cypress, and the two circles of light were just visible through the trees, about a hundred yards ahead.

"Hey, Woodburn," he said. "You left the lights on in my truck, I'm gonna kill you."

Woodburn stopped and looked at the lights. "Man, I didn't leave your lights on," he said. There was a high-pitched buzzing near his right ear, and he brushed at it with the sleeve of his Carhartt jacket. "We ain't even over there." He lifted his arm again and pointed off to the right. "We're over there."

Mooney's dog, a fawn-colored Ladner Black Mouth cur, went to tugging on his leash. Mooney tensed up on the leash and made a sound almost like he was getting something out of his teeth. The dog stopped, and the leash got some slack to it again. Mooney stopped, too.

"Those lights is about out," he said. "Somebody's gonna be pissed when they get back to their vehicle."

Woodburn looked over at him as he jerked slightly on his own leash. His brown and white Beagle stood stiffly where he was, looking toward the truck.

"Reckon we should go shut his lights off for him?" Woodburn asked.

"If the fool left his doors unlocked," Mooney answered.

"Man, this is right around where we heard that shot a while back," Woodburn said, his voice slightly hushed.

Mooney stopped walking. His dog and then his friend followed suit.

"That don't necessarily mean nothin'," Mooney said quietly.

"Maybe we should just go to your truck and call the police or somethin'," Woodburn whispered.

"Man, we got two guns," Mooney said. "Besides, what are we gonna tell 'em? Haul y'all asses out here to shut this fool's lights off? You watch too much TV."

He made a clicking noise with his tongue, and men and dogs veered off their intended path and headed for the lights. When they were about fifty feet out, Mooney squinted at the pickup that sat silently in the clearing. From where they STOOD they were looking at the truck head on. The driver's side door was standing open. The interior light either didn't work or had already burned out.

"I know that truck," Mooney said under his breath.

It was a black Ford F-150, which in Gulf County was like saying its name was John. But the Gators antenna topper was ringing a bell for Mooney.

"Whose is it?" Woodburn asked.

"Hold on, I'm thinking," Mooney answered. He was quiet for a moment. "That's Sheriff Hutchins' truck."

"Are you sure?" his friend asked him.

"Yeah, man, I put a new tranny in it last year," Mooney answered.

"Aw, man, I don't like it," Woodburn said. His beagle, Trot, had set to whining.

"I'm not real excited, either," Mooney said. "But maybe he needs help or somethin'."

"Not from us, man," Grant said. "Maybe from the cops."

"Man, pull your pants up," Mooney said. "Norman, let's go," he said to his dog, and started following him slowly into the clearing.

Mooney and Norman were in the lead, Woodburn and Trot lagging a bit behind, which was definitely Woodburn's choice and not the dog's. The beagle strained at his leash.

As Mooney got closer, he realized that the weird shininess on the driver's side window wasn't some trick of the light. Something on the window, all over it. He stopped walking. A thin sheet of moisture had suddenly appeared on his onyx skin, and he swiped at it with one huge, calloused hand.

"Sheriff?" he called out, flicking his flashlight on and off against the windshield. The flashlight wasn't a particularly powerful one. Its light bounced off the glass, revealing nothing. "Hey, Sheriff? It's Mooney White!"

The crickets and frogs went silent. For a few moments, there was just the wind in the trees and the quiet keening of the dogs.

"Shut up, Norman!" Mooney snapped, and both dogs quieted. A new sound, a faint one, reached Mooney's ears. "You hear that?"

Both men listened for a moment. "Radio," Woodburn whispered finally.

"Hell's up in here?" Mooney asked himself mostly.

He flicked the flashlight on again, trained it at the open door. In the edge of the light, he saw something, and dropped the beam lower. Beneath the door, he saw pants. Knees of pants. And one hand just hanging there.

"Aw hell, man," Woodburn whispered. "This ain't right at all."

Mooney slid his rifle down his arm, released the safety with his flashlight hand. The light bobbed off to the side of the truck.

"Sheriff?" Mooney called again. "Scarin' Mooney just a little bit here."

There was no answer. Norman gave out a couple of barks, higher-pitched than some people would expect from such a sturdy dog. Mooney gave him his lead, and followed Norman as the dog pulled toward the truck.

Mooney tugged him off to the side, made him circle wide, about eight or ten feet from the old Ford. He could hear Woodburn several yards behind him, whispering to himself.

When Mooney had gotten round to the back side of the open door, he pointed the flashlight at it.

"Oh, hellfire," Mooney said to himself.

Sheriff Hutchins was slumped forward on his knees, his upper body hung up on the open door. Closer up, the black on the window wasn't black at all, but a deep red, and there was a lot more of it on the inside of the door.

Mooney stood there staring, barely hearing his best friend gagging behind him, or Lynyrd Skynrd on the Sheriff's truck radio, singing about going home.

TWO

The cell phone bleated, vibrated, and did a little jig on the built-in teak nightstand. Evan Caldwell reached over and thumbed the answer button without looking at the screen.

"This is Vi," a deep voice intoned before he had a chance to speak.

"So it would seem," Evan answered. She always said it like that, deliberately and with brevity, like a newscaster introducing himself.

"You need to get out to Wewa," she said. "It's very serious."

"I'm off today, Vi," he said.

"Not anymore," she said, her voice like gravel that had been soaked in lye. "We need you to get out there immediately."

"I don't think that I actually know where it is," he said.

"You may not know how to pronounce Wewahitchka, but certainly you can recognize it on a map," she replied.

"Take 71 straight to Wewa. Go to the Shell station at the intersection of 71 and 22. You'll be met by Chief Beckett."

"Is he an Indian chief?"

He heard Vi try to sigh quietly. She was Sheriff Hutchins' assistant, and had apparently been with the Sheriff's Office since law enforcement was invented. Evan had only been there a few weeks and had yet to make a good impression on her. Granted, he hadn't put forth much effort. It seemed rather pointless, considering he was from "out of town" and would probably be gone again before she could decide if she liked him.

"He is the Chief of Police in Wewa," she said. "Lieutenant Caldwell, this is a very grave matter, which I don't want to explain over the phone. Chief Beckett will fill you in, then lead you to the scene."

Evan was mostly awake at this point, and her voice told him that his sarcasm would be unappreciated and possibly inappropriate.

"Did the Sheriff ask you to call me?" he asked her as he sat up.

There was silence on her end for a moment. When she finally spoke, he thought maybe her voice cracked just a little. "Please just go, as quickly as possible," she said, and hung up.

Evan looked at his phone for a moment, then checked the time. It was just after four in the morning. He swung his legs over the side of the bed and rubbed at his face as the teak sole of the master stateroom chilled his feet.

Evan was just shy of forty-two and starting to collect tiny lines at the corners of his eyes and crease lines along the sides of his mouth. His eyes were a bright, clear green that was surprising beneath his black hair and thick eyelashes. The very narrow, white scar that ran from the left corner of his mouth down to his chin kept him from being too pretty, or so his wife Hannah liked to say.

He stood up, took two steps over to the hanging locker beside his bed. One of the many reasons he'd chosen the 1986 Chris-Craft Corinthian over some of the other boats he'd seen was that it had a master stateroom with an actual bed and some halfway decent storage. Evan hadn't kept much when he'd emptied the Cocoa Beach house and moved aboard the boat, but he liked everything to have a place, and to be there when he expected it to be.

He opened the locker, pulled a pair of black trousers from their hanger and slipped them on. Three identical pairs remained in the locker, next to three identical navy trousers and five identical white button-down shirts. As he bent to step into his pants, he swore he could smell cat urine. His upper lip twitched as he leaned into the locker and sniffed. The only light in the room came from the lights on the dock, shining vague and gray through the curtains over the portholes.

His shoes, two pairs of black dress shoes, one pair of Docksiders, and a pair of running shoes, were lined up neatly on a shelf at the bottom of the locker. He bent lower, and the scent magnified. He picked up a shoe from the middle, a left dress shoe. The inside was shinier than it ought to be. He brought it to his nose and jerked back.

He managed to stop himself from throwing the shoe across the room, distributing cat pee throughout his cabin, but just barely. Instead, he carefully set it down on the floor, and pulled a shirt from the locker.

Once he had dressed, he walked in his sock feet into the boat's one head, which the previous owner had fortuitously remodeled just before he got divorced and had to sell. The guy had expanded it into the space that had been a closet, which gave him room to put in a real shower, and a space for a stacking washer and dryer. It only fit the type that people used in RVs, but it was enough for Evan, who had trouble using public appliances and would prefer buying new clothes every week to going to a laundromat.

Evan grabbed his cleaning tote from the top of the small dryer, wet a cloth with a mixture of warm water and the expensive wood soap, stalked back to the hanging locker, and thoroughly cleaned and dried the small, sloped shelf on which he kept his shoes. Then he carried the wet shoe up to the galley, tied it up in a trash bag, and set the trash bag just outside the French door to the large sun deck.

When he came back inside, he spotted the cat sitting on the built-in teak cabinet between the steps down to the V-berth Evan used for storage and the steps down to the galley. Plutes was as black as ebony and weighed at least fifteen pounds. Hannah had brought him home just a few weeks before Evan's life had fallen apart, and said she'd named him Pluto. Plutes for short.

Evan had thought she'd named him after the idiot dog from Disney. In fact, she'd taken the name from a Poe story. Evan didn't read Poe's stories, although he liked The Raven quite a bit, so he could never remember which story it was, but he thought the name was probably appropriate anyway.

The cat had never made a sound in all the time Evan had been burdened with him; at least none that Evan had been there to hear. He was a shiny, black statue of seething disdain and discontent. He turned away from one of the windows that wrapped around the entire salon and stared at Evan over his shoulder, his eyes narrowed and dismissive.

"Was that you?" Evan asked the cat, then cringed at the realization that he had become one of those people who asked cats questions. It was also a stupid question, since Plutes was the only cat aboard.

Plutes blinked at Evan, just once, slowly. Then he looked back out the window. If he could sigh, he clearly would have.

"Do it again and you'll go to the pound," Evan said, then went down the three steps that led to the eat-in galley. It was small but got good light from the windows in the salon, and it suited Evan's needs. To one side was the U-shaped galley itself, with fairly new stainless appliances and two feet of gray Corian countertop that was just enough. On the other side, a built-in dinette booth with blue striped upholstery and a small window.

Evan poured a cup of milk two thirds full and set it in the microwave to heat, then loaded up his espresso machine and turned it on. Vi had sounded distressed, and no doubt the call was urgent, but Evan had only had three hours of sleep. He wouldn't get to We-whatever any faster by crashing.

While the espresso brewed, Evan walked back to his stateroom and retrieved the undefiled dress shoes from the locker. He slipped these on, then opened a side table drawer, and pulled out his holster, his badge and his Sheriff's Office ID. He dropped the ID wallet into his pocket, clipped the holster over his belt on the right side, and fastened his badge to the front of his belt on the left.

There was a decent breeze coming through the open windows, and the air smelled briny and clean simultaneously. Evan took a deep lungful of it and mourned the day out on the water that he'd had planned. Then he went back to the galley, poured the milk and espresso into his travel mug, and took three swallows before he headed back up to the salon.

He returned Plutes' look of disgust as he crossed the salon, then stepped out onto the sun deck. It was Evan's favorite part of the boat, large enough for a rattan table and chairs and a decent stainless BBQ. He picked up the trash bag containing the stinking shoe and walked it out to a garbage can on the dock. Then he headed down the long dock toward the main marina building, now mostly dark, and the lights of Port St. Joe, FL. It was mostly dark, too.

Aside from the creaking of fenders against the dock and the clinking of mast rigging on the few sailboats nearby, the sound of Evan's footfalls was the only noise that disturbed the infant morning.

You can get *Dead Reckoning* on Amazon and read for free on Kindle Unlimited.

A NOTE FROM
THE AUTHOR

Thank you for spending some time with these characters, and this place, that I love so much.

If you'd like to be the first to know about the next book in the series, other new releases, or events and appearances, please sign up for my newsletter, *UnForgotten*, at dawnleemckenna.com

If you've missed any of the previous books in the series, you can find them all right here.

You can also hang out with myself and other readers on the Dawn Lee McKenna Facebook page. We have a lot of fun over there. Get a little nuts. You know.

If you've missed any of the books in this series, my first book, See You, or the books in the new spin-off series about Wyatt's friend Evan Caldwell, you can find them right here.

I'd like to thank all of the real people in Apalach who, generously and with good humor, have allowed me to turn them into fictional characters. Many thanks to John Solomon, Linda Joseph, Kirk and Faith Lynch, Chase Richards (otherwise known as Richard Chase), and

Officer Shawn Chisolm, as well as to Mayor Van Johnson, Sheriff AJ Smith, the Apalachicola Police Department, and the Franklin County Sheriff's Office. All of you make these books something I could not make them on my own.

As always, so much gratitude to God, to my family, and to my friends, who put up with me so that I can write, and last but not least, to the most amazing readers any writer could hope to find. I love you all.

83884779R00144

Made in the USA
San Bernardino, CA
01 August 2018